Jake Stellar

Excited About Nothing

Jake Stellar

Excited About Nothing

By
Rodney Riesel

Published by Island Holiday Publishing
East Greenbush, NY

Special thanks to:

Pamela Guerriere

Kevin Cook

Cover Image and Design by:

Connie Fitsik

To learn about my other books friend me at

https://www.facebook.com/rodneyriesel

For Brenda,
Kayleigh, Ethan
& Peyton

Chapter One

It was a beautiful Monday late morning in North Myrtle Beach. Not a cloud in the sky, and the temperature was a perfect seventy-five degrees. A light breeze off the water made it feel a little cooler than it actually was. It was perfect days like this one that inspired Bree and me, while on vacation, to move down here from New York over twelve years ago. I had the driver's side window down and my arm hung out over the door as my partner, Avis Lint, and I zipped down North Kings Highway in the department's unmarked Dodge Charger. I hummed "Margaritaville" in my head and tapped my thumb to the beat on the outside of the door. The morning sun was bright enough to make me squint my eyes even behind the protection of my aviators.

I remembered back to the first time I drove down North King's Highway. Bree and I had only been married a little over two years. Our son Ricky hadn't been born yet. We had arrived in North Myrtle for our first vacation here. It was after dark, and every five dollar or less surf shop and souvenir store was lit up with multiple colors of neon. It was like North Myrtle's very own Las Vegas Strip.

"We're coming up on the turn," said Lint, snapping me out of my reverie.

"Huh? What?" I replied foggily.

"You need to make a left up ahead."

"Yeah, okay. Guess I got lost in the past."

"Happens to the best of us."

Lint and I had cleared our caseload on Thursday and we both took a vacation day on Friday. The two of us spent all day Friday at Lint's girlfriend's camp; it was a great day of fishing. Clearing a caseload was something you never did in the Bronx—where Bree and I were from—but in North Myrtle Beach, we did it every once in a while.

Today we were helping out Detectives Gwen Lawrence and Dill Perkins with a case they were working on.

I flipped on the blinker and turned into a small trailer park that sat between the Plantation Pancake House and The Little River Fishing Fleet office. When I say small, I mean very small. There are only about fifteen trailers in the park. I pulled off the one-lane street the best I could and shut off the engine.

"Where do we start?" Lint asked. He was squinting and shading his eyes with his hand.

"Where's your sunglasses?" I asked.

"Forgot them at home."

I pushed my sunglasses up the bridge of my nose with my index finger. "That's too bad," I ribbed. I pointed across the park at a large, shirtless man in blue jeans. He was painting an old Dodge truck with a gallon can of black Rust-Oleum, using a three-inch roller.

As we approached the man, I took out my badge; Lint did the same.

"Excuse me," I said. "I'm Detective Jake Stellar, and this is my partner, Detective Avis Lint."

The guy didn't turn around. I wasn't even sure if he heard me or not. He continued to roll paint on the driver's side fender. Lint and I stood there for a second staring at his hairy back. It looked like his metamorphosis from human to lycanthrope had been halted somewhere midstream.

"We're from the North Myrtle Beach Police Department," I continued. "We were wondering if we could ask you a few questions."

Still nothing.

Lint and I looked at each other and then back at the hirsute do-it-yourselfer.

"Are you deaf, asshole?" Lint said, a little louder than I thought he should have. He brushed back his sport coat and placed his hand on his weapon. He stepped forward and put his other hand on the big guy's shoulder. "Hey."

The guy spun around, hitting Lint in the side of the face with the paint roller. It was at that exact moment I caught sight of the man's two hearing aids.

Shit, I thought. I leapt forward to get between Lint and his surprised opponent.

Lint was drawing his weapon.

"No!" I shouted, grabbing his hand. I put my hand on the deaf guy's chest and pushed him backwards; I was trying my best to get him to see the badge I was still holding. I made eye contact with him. "Look—police! Police!"

The man quickly put up his hands and Lint backed down. He rubbed the sticky oil-based paint on the side of his face and looked down at his hand. "Goddammit!" he shouted. "What the hell?"

I tried my hardest not to laugh; it was tough.

"Wannoo you gnuys wan?" asked the guy, his hands still in the air. "Wan in I do?" he fiddled with his hearing aids to turn them up.

"You didn't do anything," I said. "We just wanted to ask you a few questions."

"In none anser quesntions?"

"What?" Lint asked.

"I none anser quentions."

"You don't answer questions?" I asked.

He shook his head no.

"What's your name?" Lint asked.

"I none anser quentions. Am I fwee to ngo?"

"Seriously?" Lint asked. "Do you have any identification on you?"

"I none anser—"

"Listen, Lou Ferrigno—"

"Lint," I scolded.

He shut up, turned around, and took a deep breath. He whispered, "Well, the guy is being an asshole." He continued to paw at the black paint on his face.

"Everyone's an asshole nowadays," I whispered back. "Thank you for your time, sir." I turned and started toward another trailer house.

The guy returned his attention to his masterful auto body work.

"What the hell is wrong with people?" Lint asked. He followed close behind me. "I don't answer questions. Am I free to go? Am I being detained? I know my rights."

"Everyone's a Facebook attorney," I said.

"I hope the guy who invented YouTube gets hit by a bus," Lint mumbled.

We walked up some steps and onto an old front deck that looked as though it might not support us. I knocked on the door. I was still holding my badge.

The front door opened and a pale, skinny woman with a black eye and a few black teeth asked, "What do you want?"

I flashed my badge and told her who we were.

"What do you want?" she asked again.

"We were wondering if we could ask you a few questions," Lint said.

"Sure," she replied, "go ahead."

"Can we step inside?" I asked.

"No," she said. "Y'all got any questions, you can ask 'em right where ya stand." She removed the cigarette from her mouth and coughed a few times. The rattle in her lungs sounded like an idling semi. When she had coughed up and swallowed everything she had in her chest, she put the cigarette back between her lips and took a big drag.

I pointed back at the trailer that sat next door to the deaf guy. "The white van that was parked in that driveway last—"

"Didn't know them," she interrupted.

"Do you know how long the van had been sitting—"

"Didn't notice."

"Why don't you let him finish his sentence?" Lint asked angrily.

"Because it don't matter if he finishes the sentence or not," she replied. "I don't know whose van it was. I don't know how long it sat there. I don't even know the people who lived in that trailer. Y'all can ask as many questions as ya wont. Ain't nobody in this park gonna give ya the answers you're lookin' fer."

"So you're saying you don't—"

"Time's up," she said, and slammed the door in my face.

I knocked a few more times, but she didn't answer. We turned and walked off the deck.

"I hate people," said Lint.

"It's the only thing we have in common, partner," I said.

We spent the next forty-five minutes in the trailer park knocking on doors, asking questions, and getting pretty much the same answers we had gotten from the lunger.

When we returned to the car and drove out of the park, Lint said, "I hope we get a case tomorrow. I'm sick of doing Perkins and Gwen's legwork."

"Yeah, me too," I agreed sarcastically. "What we need is a good violent crime."

Lint had pulled a napkin out of the glove box and was vigorously wiping at the paint on his cheek. "Goddammit," he said.

"It's gonna take more than an old Sonic napkin to get that paint off," I said.

"What should I use?"

"You'll probably need paint thinner."

"If I ever see that bastard again …"

Chapter Two

I got home from work around four thirty that afternoon; Bree had the day off. I parked in the driveway, hit the garage door opener that was clipped to my visor, and walked in through the garage. I took off my jacket and hung it on the back of the kitchen chair. I glanced down at the two small bowls on the floor next to the cupboard; one was full of water and the other contained dry dog food. I walked over and looked into the living room. Our miniature Yorkie, Woofie, was sound asleep on the couch.

After searching the entire house for Bree, a note taped to the front of the microwave told me she had walked down to the beach, and for me to walk down if I wanted to. I didn't want to, but I put on a pair of cargo shorts, a black T-shirt, and went any way; I carried a can of ginger ale with me.

With my flip-flops flip-flopping, I walked down Hillside Drive, took a left, and walked the four blocks to the Twenty-Seventh Avenue beach access path. When I got to the end of the path, Bree was standing in the sand folding her towel. When she finished, she bent over, removed a T-shirt from her beach bag, and pulled it on over her head. She picked up the bag and towel, and headed toward me. When she saw me she gave a slight wave, but there was no smile with it; that was odd for Bree.

"What's the matter?" I asked, when she reached me.

Bree pointed back in the opposite direction as she breezed past me. "Those kids kept saying shit," she remarked bitterly over her shoulder.

"Saying shit like what?" I asked, flip-flopping along to catch up.

"Stupid shit guys say."

"Like what?"

"One commented on my ass, and another one said something about my boobs and that he liked older women."

I started toward the young men, who were probably only in their late teens. Vacationing with their folks, no doubt, and staying at one of the beachfront motels. Bree turned quickly and grabbed me by the wrist. "No!" she said. "Don't say anything."

"I'm going to say something." I tried to pull away, but Bree's grip was strong. She tightened her hand around my wrist.

"Really, don't. I shouldn't have said anything."

"Not saying anything doesn't mean it didn't happen."

"Come on. Let's go home."

I looked back at the teens standing in the sand. They were staring back at me. They wanted me to come back and say something. I studied each asshole's face, hoping I would see them again somewhere. I looked back at Bree.

"Please," she said.

"Fine." I turned and we held hands and started back up the access path. I took her beach bag from her and threw it up over my shoulder. "This goes against everything I believe in."

"Carrying my bag?"

"Not saying anything to those assholes."

"That's right, old man!" one of the kids shouted.

I felt my shoulders stiffen but I ignored him. Instead, I fantasized about going up to the little bastard's motel room and beating the shit out of his father. I glanced back over my shoulder to make a mental note of their board shorts, hairstyles, and builds. Who knows, if I'm lucky I may run into them again.

Bree was quiet most of the way home.

"You okay?" I asked, when we got to our driveway.

"Yeah," she replied. "I think what bothered me the most is when the little prick said he liked older women."

I shook my head. "Of course it did."

We walked up the horseshoe driveway that faced Hillside Drive and went inside. I dropped Bree's bag near the front door.

"So how was your day?" Bree asked.

"It was pretty good," I replied, "right up until we had to question some people at a trailer park."

"Which trailer park?"

"That dumpy park next to Plantation Pancake House."

Bree nodded in recognition of the place. "Not very helpful?"

I went into the living room and took a seat in my recliner. "Most of them chose to invoke their Fifth Amendment privilege and not so respectfully declined to answer our questions." I picked up the remote control and turned the television, which was already on, to the Weather Channel.

"A man's got to know his rights," said Bree.

"Yeah," I agreed. "That's what Facebook taught them."

Bree went down the hall to the bedroom and returned a few minutes later wearing frayed denim shorts with a small hole in one leg that revealed part of her front pocket. She sat down on the couch next to Woofie. "How's Mommy's widdew baby?" she asked.

"Mommy's widdew baby is starving," I said.

"There was food in her bowl."

"I was talking about me."

"Oh. What should we do for dinner?"

"That's up to you."

"You decide," Bree insisted. "You know I'm not choosy."

"Here we go," I mumbled.

"What's that supposed to mean?"

"You know what it means. I'm going to suggest about ten places and you'll say no to every one of them, and then we'll go where you wanted to in the first place."

"Yeah, right. How often does that happen?"

"Every damn time."

"Whatever. I'll go get ready." She stood and made her way down the hall.

"I'd like to leave by six," I called out to her.

"It's only five," she called back.

"Exactly."

"It doesn't take me an hour to get ready. You're a jerk."

"We'll see."

At ten after six we left the house to get something to eat.

Chapter Three

Around ten o'clock that same night Bree was curled up on the couch with a blanket thrown over her, and Woofie snuggled up next to her. I was in my recliner, fully reclined, and half asleep. A glass with ice and ginger ale sat on the end table next to me. My cell phone sat next to it.

We were watching a Lifetime movie called *Deadly Delusion*. Bree was really into the movie, like she is with most Lifetime movies. For me, the only good part about the film was Haylie Duff, the better looking of the Duff sisters. She's appeared in about a million Lifetime movies, and I think I've seen them all. Yeah, I've seen her go through a lot of shit in the past few years. She's been beaten up, she's lost her memory, and she's had more than one husband try to murder her. She's one tough woman.

I reached over to grab my glass just as my cell phone rang and scared the shit out of me. I swear, the older I get, the jumpier I get.

"Stellar," I said.

"Jake, it's Gwen. We've got a hostage situation at 4947 South Island Drive."

"I'm on my way."

Bree sat up and turned the volume down on the television. "Everything okay?" she asked.

I put down the foot rest and climbed out of my chair. "Got something going on over on Island Drive." I grabbed my shoes and slipped them on.

"Be careful."

"Always am." I leaned over and kissed Bree on the lips.

"Love you," she said.

"Love you too," I replied. I nodded my head in the direction of the TV. "Hit record, will ya? I won't be able to sleep tonight if I don't know Haylie's going to be okay."

"Get out of here."

Ten minutes later I took a right onto Inlet Way. I could see the flashing lights at the end of the street. I pulled my truck to the curb behind an ambulance, got out, and walked the last twenty yards or so. I carried my bulletproof vest with me. There were two patrol cars blocking the end of Inlet Way; an officer stood near each unit. There were six patrol cars sitting up and down Island Drive; all with their light bars flashing. Several officers had taken positions behind them.

I flashed my gold shield. "What do we got?" I asked.

One of the officers turned and pointed at the subject's house on Island Drive, directly across from the end of Inlet Way. "Guy called 911," the officer said. "Caller said he got home from work and saw his wife being attacked."

Detective Lint was now beside me.

"No one has entered the residence?" I asked.

"No."

"Why not?" Lint asked.

Just then Detective Gwen Lawrence walked up to us. She was wearing blue jeans, a navy blue T-shirt, and sneakers. She was also wearing her tactical vest that said police across the front in white letters. "Hope I didn't interrupt anything important," she said.

"No," I replied. "It was just a Lifetime movie."

"Was it the new one with Haylie Duff?"

"Yeah."

"Dammit. I wanted to see that."

"I was already in bed," said Lint.

"So, what's going on here?" I asked. "Why has no one gone in?"

"The homeowner, Doug Oliver, told the dispatcher that his wife, Jennifer, was being assaulted by a man with a knife," Gwen explained. "Then the phone went dead. When the first unit arrived they tried to make contact. That's when a male inside the residence hollered out one of the windows, 'Anyone tries to come in here, these two are dead — or something to that effect. Nothing after that."

"What time did the 911 call come in?"

"Nine thirty-five."

I looked at my watch. "Thirty-eight minutes. Negotiator on the way?"

"He's already here." Gwen pointed at another unit about twenty feet down Island Drive.

A tall, thin man I recognized as Glenn Lembeck stood behind the patrol car. The bullhorn in his right hand dangled at his side.

At the exact moment I heard the SWAT van's engine rev behind me, four shots rang out. Everyone in the area flinched and took cover. All eyes were on the house.

The SWAT van squealed to a halt.

The front door of the house swung open. A man in khakis and a gray shirt exited the house; he held a pistol in his hand.

I drew my pistol. So did Lint and Gwen.

"Drop your weapon!" Lembeck shouted into the bullhorn. "Drop your weapon!"

"My wife—I think he killed her!" the man shouted. He let go of the revolver and it hit the grass.

"Get on the ground!" hollered Lembeck.

SWAT officers dressed in full tactical gear were running past me.

The gunman got on his knees, but before he was all the way to the ground he was swarmed by several officers who shoved him down and cuffed him.

SWAT was at the open front door. They entered the home. Lint and I trotted toward the house.

Less than a minute later, Sergeant Pinky Brady—the SWAT team leader—was back at the front door. "All secure!" he shouted, and holstered his SIG Sauer P220.

Two officers put the gunman in the backseat of one of the patrol cars. Lint and I holstered our weapons and went inside the house.

We walked through the front door, into the living room, down a hallway, and into a bedroom. A naked black man in his mid-to-late forties lay on his back on the floor, next to the bed, with three gunshot wounds to his chest. Next to the man's right hand was a bloody knife. I looked at the wall behind where the dead man would have been standing when shot. There was a bullet hole in the sheetrock.

On the bed was a dark-haired Caucasian woman around the same age as the dead man. She was also naked. Her feet and hands were bound to the bedposts with pantyhose. She had several stab wounds to her torso. She was covered in blood and so were the blankets underneath her.

This was the point in an investigation when Lint usually said something really stupid and inappropriate. The brutality of the scene must have left him at a loss for words, because he said nothing. I didn't know how many times in the past he had seen something like this, but for me, I hadn't since leaving the Bronx.

A pair of pants lay folded neatly on an accent chair. A man's white T-shirt was folded and laying on top of the pants. Underneath the edge of the chair was a pair of flip-flops. I walked over to the pants and checked the back pocket for a wallet. Finding it, I removed it and looked at the driver's license. The license belonged to the dead man. His name was Ronald L. Mosley, forty-eight years old, and he lived in North Myrtle Beach at 4608 Woodland Street. I closed the wallet and placed it back in the pocket.

Tom Powers, a medical examiner with the Horry County Coroner's Office, was next through the door. Tom was only five foot one, and with his boyish face and blond hair parted on the side, he looked like every altar boy in every movie about the Catholic Church.

"Oh my," Tom said.

When the ME says "Oh my," you know it's bad.

Tom placed his black leather medical bag on the mirrored dresser next to an empty bottle of wine. "Husband?" he asked, staring down at the body.

"No," I replied. "The husband's outside."

A crime scene photographer entered the room and immediately started taking pictures.

Lint was still scanning the room and taking in the entire crime scene when I nudged him and said, "Let's get out of these guy's way."

We passed two other members of the Crime Scene Unit in the hall on our way back outside. We nodded and they nodded back.

Outside, Detective Lawrence was standing at a patrol car speaking to the husband through an open rear window.

"Let him out," I said, as I neared the unit.

Gwen opened the door and held out her hand to assist him. The front of his gray long sleeved, button down shirt was covered in blood. When I removed his handcuffs, I saw that his hands were covered in blood as well.

"Can you tell us what happened, Mr. Oliver?" I asked.

"My wife *is* dead, isn't she?" he asked.

"I'm afraid so," I said.

His face went ashen. "How could she not be? All those horrible stab wounds ..." He didn't finish the thought. "Is Ron dead?"

I nodded.

"You know your wife's attacker?" Lint asked.

"Yes," said Doug.

"Did your wife know him as well?" I asked.

Doug continued to stare at the ground. He nodded his head slowly. "They worked together."

"Where did Jennifer work, Doug?" I asked.

"She was the nurse at the high school."

"North Myrtle Beach High School?" Lint asked.

"Yes," Doug replied.

"*Was* the nurse?" I asked.

"She was fired a couple months ago."

"Why was she let go?" I asked.

"They claimed she made false statements about a coworker."

"And the coworker was—"

"Ron Mosley," said Doug.

I looked around for the nearest of the two ambulances on site. "You've got a lot of blood on you, Doug. Why don't you walk with Detective Lint and me over to the ambulance and have a paramedic take a quick look at you?"

Doug looked at his hands and the front of his shirt. "It's not my blood," he said.

"I know," I said, "but I would feel better if they checked you out."

Doug Oliver walked across South Island Drive with us and down Inlet Way to the ambulance. I pointed at the back of the ambulance. "Have a seat right here, Doug."

Doug sat on the back bumper. He kept trying to look past us at the house, and his eyes settled on the coroner's van. "They're not going to put the two of them in the same vehicle, are they?" he asked. His voice shook.

"We'll make sure they don't," I told him.

A paramedic jumped out of the back of the ambulance and began checking Doug's arms, neck, and head for injuries. Doug continued craning his neck for a better view of his house.

"Explain to us exactly what happened when you arrived home tonight," I said.

Doug buried his face in his hands and began sobbing uncontrollably. "Can ... we ... do this later?" he asked. He started to stand and stumbled backwards against the ambulance. "I feel light headed."

"Sit back down," the paramedic instructed. He looked at Lint and me. "The adrenaline is wearing off. He's in shock. Help me get him into the back."

I put my arm under Doug's arm and the paramedic did the same. Together we helped him up into the ambulance and laid him down on a gurney.

"I'm going to start an IV," said the paramedic.

I patted Doug on the shin and gave it a squeeze. "We'll be in touch tomorrow, Doug."

"Very sorry for your loss," Lint added.

I jumped out of the back of the ambulance. I turned and watched as the paramedic took Doug's vitals. Lint and I turned and started back down Inlet Way.

"Poor bastard," Lint commented.

"I can't even imagine," I said.

Lint pulled his cell phone out of his front pocket. "I'm going to give Bertie a call and tell her I'll be a few hours.

"Good idea," I said, and reached for my own cell.

Chapter Four

I didn't get home until two the following morning. I slept for three hours and then Bree woke me up when she got out of bed. It was going to be a long day.

"Go back to sleep," Bree said.

"That's not going to happen." I responded. "Too much on my mind."

"Last night?" she asked.

"Yeah." I threw my legs over the edge of the bed and slid my feet into my house shoes.

Bree removed her robe off the hook on the back of the bedroom door. "What time did you come in?"

"Around two."

"I didn't even hear you."

I exited the room behind Bree. She walked across the hall into the guest bedroom that I had long ago turned into a giant closet for her. I turned and walked down the hall to the kitchen. I pushed the Kuerig's power button and grabbed two cups out of the cupboard above it. I placed one of the cups under the Kuerig and popped a blueberry-flavored K-cup into the slot. I pressed the lever down and hit the "large cup" button.

The gurgling of the Kuerig always gets things moving first thing in the morning. I waited in much discomfort as the cup slowly filled. When it had filled halfway, it was all I could take, I pulled out my cup and slid the empty cup underneath the coffee stream. I turned and hurried with my coffee as quickly as I could down the hall to the bathroom, squeezing my butt cheeks together as I shuffled. *Just in time!*

When I walked out of the bathroom, I could hear the shower running in Bree's bathroom. I returned to the coffee maker and added the coffee from the other cup into my own cup, then I made Bree a cup.

By the time I got to the bathroom with Bree's cup of coffee, she was already out of the shower, dried off, and was back in her robe. *Dammit! Wasn't quick enough.* I know Bree thinks I make her coffee and bring it to her in the bathroom because I'm a nice guy. The truth is, I bring it in there just to see her naked first thing in the morning. Seeing her naked is the perfect way to start my day. I sat the cup on the vanity.

"Thank you," she said.

"Whatcha got under that robe?" I asked.

"Same thing I had under there yesterday morning."

"Prove it."

She cocked her head and gave me the stare. "Really?"

"I brought you coffee," I deadpanned.

She turned toward me and opened the robe. "Good enough?'

"Yup."

She closed the robe. I kissed her on the lips, and then went to hunt for the morning paper.

I found the morning edition of the Sun News lodged in one of the two forsythia bushes that Bree had to have for her birthday last year. I had to admit the bell-shaped yellow flowers were a beautiful harbinger of spring, but the prolific bushes themselves would swallow the house if I didn't keep them cut back. I tossed the paper on the table when I got back inside.

I looked around the room. *What the hell did I do with my coffee?* I wondered. Luckily, before I went insane, Bree walked into the kitchen holding her cup and mine.

"You left this in the bedroom," Bree informed me.

"Thanks," I said. I took a seat at the table and opened up the newspaper. Nothing about last night's homicide, must have happened too late.

"You want anything for breakfast?" Bree asked.

"What are you making?"

"What do you want?"

"Pancakes and sausage."

"I'm making scrambled eggs and bacon."

"Then why did you ask?"

"Just to get your hopes up and then crush them."

"Wow, that's heartless."

"I'm a cold woman, Jake Stellar."

Woofie heard the word breakfast—one of the seven or eight words she recognizes—and moseyed into the kitchen. "It's scrambled eggs and bacon," I told her.

Woofie stopped, stared at me for a second, gave Bree a look, turned, and went back into the living room.

"She wanted pancakes too," I said.

"Did Mommy's baby want pancakes?" Bree baby-talked, while laying the bacon in the frying pan one strip at a time.

I sipped my coffee and went back to the funnies.

Bree diced up some onion and green pepper and fried it up in a pan before adding the eggs she had beaten. "Toast?" she asked.

"Uh-huh," I replied.

When she finished making our plates she set one in front of me and placed the other where she usually sat.

"Yum," I said. She had also melted pre-shredded Swiss cheese on top of the scrambled eggs.

"So, what went on last night?" Bree asked.

I didn't like getting into too much detail with Bree when it came to my work. Bree was the type of person who worried about everything and thought way too much about everything. She always asked, however, and every little bit of information I would give her would always lead to question after question, and before you knew it, I had given her too much detail.

"You sure you want to hear about this?" I asked.

"How bad is it?" she asked.

"Not as bad as some, but worse than most," I said. "The scene was bad."

"What happened?"

"A guy over on Island Drive came home and found another man murdering his wife."

"Eesh."

"Yeah, eesh."

"Is the husband okay?"

"As okay as you can be after seeing something like that."

"Did you catch the perp? Is he in jail?"

I loved it when Bree said perp. "No, the perp is dead. The husband shot him."

"Well, that's good, I guess. At least there's not a killer on the streets."

"Um … yeah."

Bree cocked an inquisitive eyebrow. "Um … yeah? What do you mean, um … yeah?"

Woofie returned to the kitchen and sat next to my chair, staring up at me. I took a bite of my bacon and then broke off a few small pieces for her. I tossed them on the floor next to her and she inhaled them.

"You gotta chew that shit up, dog," I said. "You're gonna choke."

Bree wouldn't let it go. "Why did you say 'Um … yeah' like that?"

"I don't know. Something just doesn't seem right."

"Like what?"

"Can't put my finger on it. The guy acted just like you expect him to act if something like that happened. He was even concerned that his wife and her attacker would be in the same van on the ride to the morgue."

"That makes sense."

33

"Yeah, it does."

"Then what is it?"

"I don't know. Probably nothing."

"Did you question him at the scene?"

"Not much. He wasn't in very good shape."

"Understandable."

"I guess. He's coming in today for questioning."

"Sad," Bree commented, ending the conversation. She picked up her plate. "You finished with that?"

"Yes."

She picked up my plate too and took them to the sink. She glanced at the clock on the microwave. "I better get going." We kissed and she said, "Get out there and keep us safe."

"I'll try," I replied, and she left for work.

On my way down the hall to take a shower my cell phone rang. I looked at the caller ID; it was Lint. "Yeah?" I said.

"You awake?" he asked.

"Yeah. Why?"

"I just got a call from Gwen. She said Doug Oliver is already at the station."

"For what?"

"To be interviewed, I guess."

"It's only seven o'clock."

"I guess he's anxious to give his account."

"I'll meet you there in twenty-five minutes," I said, and hung up.

Chapter Five

Lint was already sitting at his desk when I arrived at the station; Doug Oliver was sitting in a chair across from him. I walked up behind Doug and put my hand on his shoulder; it startled him a little.

Doug looked up at me. "Oh, hey," he said. His eyes were puffy and blood shot as well. He was wearing the same clothes as the night before. His hair was messy, but not what you would call bedhead.

"Have you slept at all, Doug?" I asked. I turned and went to my desk. I removed my 9mm from my shoulder holster and placed it in the top drawer.

"I fell asleep for about fifteen minutes," said Doug.

"We didn't expect you this early," I remarked.

He shrugged. "I thought it would be better if things were fresh in my mind."

I pointed at the door that led to the lounge. "Let's talk in there," I said.

Lint got up and walked to the door. He opened it and stepped back to allow Doug to enter first. "Right in here," Lint instructed.

Doug sat in one of the dark leather chairs. Lint and I sat on the matching sofa against the opposite wall. Lint crossed his legs and laid his note pad on his thigh.

"Can we get you something to drink?" Lint asked. "A cup of coffee, soda, or something?"

"No, thank you. I've had four cups of coffee in the last three hours."

"You said you had just come in from work last night?" I asked.

Doug nodded his head. "Yes. I got home around … nine thirty from work."

"Where do you work?" Lint asked.

"I'm an assistant manager at Home Depot."

"Here in North Myrtle?" I asked.

"No, the one down in Myrtle Beach."

"What happened when you arrived home?" I asked.

Doug took a deep breath and let it out slowly. "I came in the front door—"

"Was the door locked?" Lint interrupted.

Doug thought for a second. "No, I went right in. The lights were on in the living room. The TV too. Nothing unusual about that, but something just didn't feel right. You know, like when everything looks fine, but you still know something is wrong. It was just a feeling. You know what I mean? I called out Jen's name."

Doug looked to each of us for a response. Our stone-faced expressions told him to continue.

"Then I heard ... like ... a muffled sound. I walked down the hall and the bedroom door was open. It was dark in the bedroom, but still enough light that I could see what was going on. Jen was on the bed naked, and Ron was straddling her; he was naked too. He had one hand over her mouth and with the knife in his other hand he was stabbing her. She was flailing her legs all over the place, trying to free herself. He just kept stabbing her. Even when he looked over his shoulder at me ... he just kept stabbing."

Doug was unconsciously making violent thrusting motions with his balled fist. I saw the unsettled look on Lint's face and wondered if I had one to match.

"Was he saying anything?" Lint asked in a squeaky unintelligible voice. He cleared his throat and repeated the question.

"He shouted, 'This'll teach white bitches to keep their mouths shut.'"

"Dispatch said that your 911 call came in at nine thirty-five," I told him. "According to the responding officer's report—what they heard from outside, and what you explained to us, you shot Mosley at approximately ten minutes after ten. That's thirty-five minutes."

"Really?" Doug said. "It seemed a lot longer."

"What I'm asking, Doug, is what went on for thirty-five minutes?"

"Well, when Ron climbed off of Jen, he turned toward me—"

"You were still standing in the doorway?" Lint asked.

"Yes," Doug replied. "He starts coming toward me and says, 'Now it's your turn.'"

"He still had the knife in his hand?" I asked.

"Yes."

"What did you do?" Lint asked.

"I grabbed the doorknob and pulled the bedroom door closed. Then I ran for my gun. I keep it in the pantry on the top shelf, in a lockbox, unloaded. I got inside the pantry and shut the door. I could hear Ron walking around the house looking for me. I called 911 from the pantry on my cell phone. I tried to be as quiet as I could. Then, a while later, I heard Ron yell out the window at the cops, so I knew he was back in the bedroom. I took the gun out of the lock box, loaded it, and waited a little while longer."

"What were you waiting for?" Lint asked.

"I don' know. I was just scared."

"How long did you wait before you left the pantry?" I asked.

Doug shrugged his shoulders. "I don't know. Like I said, it seemed a lot longer than it actually was."

"But you finally left, and then what?" I asked.

"I went back to the bedroom."

"The bedroom door was open when you got back?" Lint asked.

"Yes," Doug said. "And Ron saw me when I came around the corner. I raised the gun. He froze. I said, 'Don't move Ron.' He said, 'I had to do it Doug. I had to do it.' He came at me with the knife, and I just started pulling the trigger until he fell."

"That's when you came outside?" I asked.

"No. First I tried to do CPR on Jen. I don't know why. It was obvious she was already dead. I didn't know what I was doing. I got off the bed and came outside." Doug dropped his head and stared at the floor. He rubbed his eyes.

Lint and I looked at each other, and then back at Doug. We gave him a minute or two to regain his composure.

"You said your wife worked with Mosley and that she had been fired for making a false accusation about him. What was that all about?" I asked.

"It started about six months ago," Doug said. "Ron wouldn't leave her alone at work."

"What do you mean, leave her alone?" Lint asked.

"It started out as off-color jokes, and then progressed into sexual comments. He would comment on what she was wearing and how her ass or breasts looked in an outfit. At first she laughed it off, but it escalated. He even cornered her in her office once. That's when she went to the principal with her complaints."

"Was Ron reprimanded?" I asked.

"They claim he was, but Ron didn't stop the harassment."

"What did Jen do next?" Lint asked.

"She contacted the superintendent and the school board. There was a meeting, and Jen was let go for making false claims."

"Why would they let your wife go?" I asked.

"Jen had only been with the school system for a little over a year. Ron was a teacher at the high school for twenty years, and they said he had a clean record. It was a classic case of he said, she said. There were no witnesses to his actions—besides Jen, I mean."

"Did your wife have a clean record?" Lint asked.

I shot him a look.

"Of course," Doug replied. "But later we found out that Ron and the superintendent—Henry Collins—had been friends for years."

"Do you know the exact date of Jen's termination?" I asked.

"Not off the top of my head. Sometime in November, right before Thanksgiving."

"Did the two of you seek legal action?" I asked.

"No."

"Why not?" Lint asked.

"Because they told us that if she left quietly and didn't pursue the matter, they would give her a positive recommendation in her job search."

"And if not, they would drag her through the mud," Lint surmised.

Doug nodded. "Exactly."

"Has your wife had any contact with Ron Mosley since she left the school?" I asked.

"There have been hang-ups, and once Jen thought he was driving by the house, but nothing we could prove."

I stood first and Lint followed. "Thank you for your time, Doug, and again, we're very sorry for your loss."

Doug stood, shook our hands, and thanked us. "If you need me for anything, I'm staying with my brother and his wife in Little River."

While Lint escorted Doug to the parking lot, I sat down at my desk and began studying the notes Lint had made.

When Lint walked back into the squad room he asked, "Well, what do you think?"

"I think Doug Oliver wrapped up this case in a tidy little ball for us."

Chapter Six

Perkins and Lawrence were still working another case, so I knew Lint and I would be doing all the legwork on this one ourselves. Our first stop was North Myrtle Beach High School.

Principal Klaudia Rothstein stood when Lint and I entered her office. It had been over a year and a half since our last visit with Ms. Rothstein—during our investigation into the death of one of her teachers, Emily Bowen. Not much had changed in that year and a half. I was still a detective, Lint was still fat, and Klaudia was still doing yoga, or following Weight Watchers, or drinking the blood of teenage virgins, or whatever it is that the hottest women in the world do to sustain their beauty.

"Good morning, Detective Stellar," said Klaudia.

"Good morning," I returned.

She looked to Lint. "And Detective Lint."

"Yes, ma'am," said Lint. He looked away. Lint always found it difficult to make eye contact with really beautiful women.

"Please, have a seat." She motioned to the two wooden chairs across from her desk.

We sat, and Klaudia sat too. She used the long red fingernail of her index finger to hook her long brown hair behind her ear. Lint was staring and his mouth was slowly opening like a fat bass about to gobble up a worm, so I kicked his foot.

"Ow!" said Lint.

Klaudia looked at him confusedly. "So, what brings you gentlemen in today?"

It had only been a few hours since the double homicide, and no names or statements had been released to the media, so there was a good chance Klaudia knew nothing about why Lint and I were there. "We're investigating the death of a past employee of yours," I informed her.

A look of seriousness washed over her, and her hand went to her chest. "Oh my goodness. Not again. Who?"

"Jennifer Oliver," I said.

"Oh, my." Klaudia leaned forward and rested her forearms on her desk and interlocked her fingers. "What happened?"

"She was murdered in her home," said Lint.

Klaudia's face turned white. "Do you know who did it?"

"Ronald Mosley," I said.

"What?" asked Klaudia. "*Our* Ronald Mosley?"

"Yes," I said.

"That's impossible!"

"Why do you say that?" I asked.

"Especially after what happened to her here a few months back," Lint added.

"Happened to her? What do you mean, *happened* to her?"

"The persistent sexual harassment Mosley subjected her to," Lint reminded her.

Klaudia wasn't letting go of her bewildered expression. She pressed a button at the bottom of her desk phone. "Andrea, can you grab Jennifer Oliver's file and bring it in here, please?" She returned her attention to us. "She only left a few months ago, but I don't recall there being any instances of harassment."

"Left?" I asked. "We were under the impression that Mrs. Oliver had been terminated."

"Well," said Klaudia, "she was asked to put in her resignation, but it had nothing to do with harassment."

The door opened, and Andrea walked in carrying a manila file folder. It didn't appear to contain much.

"Thank you, Andrea." Klaudia took the folder. Andrea nodded, smiled, and left the room. "Let's have a look here." Klaudia opened the folder and began flipping through the paperwork. "Her termination was due to poor attendance and nothing more."

I held out my hand. "May I have a look at that?" I read down through Jennifer Oliver's performance review; it was dated November 17. The only negative comments on the page were about her attendance record. I handed the paper back to Klaudia. "Can we get a copy of everything in that folder?"

"Of course."

I put on my best let's-cut-to-the-chase face and said, "Ms. Rothstein, we were told by Mrs. Oliver's husband that she had been repeatedly harassed by Ronald Mosley during her employment here, and that she had met with you on more than one occasion to discuss it."

"I don't recall anything like that ever taking place," Klaudia replied.

"We were also told that there was a meeting with the school's superintendent," said Lint.

"Henry Collins?"

I nodded. "Mr. Oliver said she was terminated by you for making false accusations about Ronald Mosley," I said.

Klaudia was slowly shaking her head no. "I don't recall any of that," she said. "That never happened. Do I need an attorney?"

Lint and I looked at each other, then back at Klaudia. "Do you feel like you need a lawyer?" I asked.

"I feel like I'm being accused of something."

"We're not accusing you of anything," said Lint.

"There's nothing in that folder about Ronald Mosley harassing Jennifer Oliver?" I asked.

"No." Klaudia handed me the entire folder. She pressed the button on her phone again. "Andrea, can you please bring me Ronald Mosley's file?"

"He didn't show up for his classes today." came Andrea's voice from the speaker.

"I know," said Klaudia. "Please get me his folder."

I stood. "We'll need copies of that folder as well," I said.

I subtly jerked my head at Lint. He rose, as did Klaudia, who led us to the front desk.

After Andrea had made copies of both files, I thanked Klaudia Rothstein once again for her help.

"Are you sure I don't need an attorney?" she asked one last time.

"Only if you want one," Lint replied.

We exited the building and headed back to the Charger; Lint carried the file folders in his hand.

"You think she's lying?" Lint asked.

"Someone is lying," I replied.

"Why would they cover up something like that?"

"Maybe because Mosley and Superintendent Collins were great pals."

"Maybe," said Lint. "But I know I'll think a lot better after a SuperSONIC Bacon Double Cheeseburger."

"Yeah," I replied. "It's been a whole two hours since you jammed those five Krispy Kremes into your pork trap."

Chapter Seven

"Do I have anything on my face?" Lint asked as we walked across the parking lot to the station.

I inspected his face. There was a smear of ketchup on his left cheek. My eyes moved down to the yellow stain on his shirt. "Nothing on your face," I said. "But there's mustard on the front of your shirt."

Lint looked down at the stain. "Dammit!"

I chuckled.

"Run me home quick so I can change my shirt," he asked.

"No," I said.

"Come on."

I pulled open the door to the squad room. "No."

"Please."

"Shut up." I opened my desk and placed my weapon in the top drawer. Lint did the same at his desk. Captain

Merle Stein's office door opened. He poked his head into the squad room.

"Stellar! Lint!" Merle hollered. "Get in here!" He disappeared back into his office.

"Are we in trouble?" Lint asked me.

"I don't think so," I replied.

I walked into Merle's office. Lint was close behind. Merle was at his desk; a cup of coffee sat to his right. A McDonald's hamburger sat on its wrapper to his left. There were two bites taken out of it. That distinctive McDonald's smell—like the underbelly of a goat—was heavy in the air.

Merle leaned back in his chair and ran his fingers through his jet black, slicked back hair. There wasn't one gray on his head. He swore it was natural. Everyone was positive he was lying, just like he lied about not going to the tanning salon. As usual he was wearing a white, buttoned-down, long-sleeved dress shirt that looked as though it had been removed from its wrapper only moments earlier.

"What's up, Cap'n?" I asked. I sat down on the sofa against the wall across from his desk.

Lint sat down on the armrest.

"Get your ass off the arm of my couch," Merle scolded.

Lint quickly stood. "Sorry."

"Did you harass and make fun of a deaf guy at a trailer park on North Kings Highway yesterday?" Merle demanded.

Lint looked around the room as though he was searching for the culprit. He looked back at Merle, "Me?" he asked, pointing at himself.

"Yeah, you," said Merle.

"Did someone say I did?" Lint asked.

"No," Merle replied. "They said a fat detective did."

"Oh."

"Well?"

"I didn't make fun of him," Lint said.

Merle leaned forward and looked at some chicken scratch on a Post-it note. "So, you didn't refer to him as Lou Ferrigno?"

"Well, yes," Lint admitted. "But it was because of his muscles."

Merle cocked his head. "How stupid do I look?"

Lint shrugged. "Not very."

"One more complaint like this and it's back to sensitivity training for you."

"Yes, sir," Lint grumbled.

Merle looked at me. "Where we at on the Oliver thing?"

"We just got back from the high school," I said. "No one seems to know anything about Ronald Mosley's sexual harassment of the victim."

"Are you thinking cover-up?"

"Too early to tell," I said.

"Is the autopsy report in yet?"

"Not yet."

Merle leaned back in his chair again. "Okay, keep me up to date," he said. "Get out of here. Oh, and, Lint—wipe that damn ketchup off your cheek. You look like a slob."

Lint and I walked out of the office and shut the door behind us.

Lint was glaring at me as he wiped his face. "Thanks for your help in there," he said.

"Help?" I asked.

"About the deaf guy," he reminded me.

"Hey, people shouldn't bully other people." I sat down at my desk. "Especially you."

Lint shot me a look. "What do you mean, especially me?"

"Well, I just meant—"

"I know what you meant. You meant because I was a fat kid."

"Well?"

"Well, nothing." Lint sat down at his desk. "I wasn't bullied as a kid. The class clown never gets bullied."

"Who was the class clown?" I asked.

"Me, asshole."

"You were the class clown?" I asked in disbelief.

"Yeah. Why?"

"Because you're not funny."

"I am too."

"No, you're not."

"Oh, and you are?"

"I think I'm pretty funny."

"You're the only one who thinks so."

"We'll agree to disagree."

"I ain't agreein' with shit."

I chuckled. "You are funny." My cell phone rang. "Stellar," I answered.

"Jake, it's Tom Powers."

"Hey, Tom. What's up?"

"I'm finishing up the Oliver autopsy and I should have the Mosley autopsy finished this afternoon. You stoppin' over, or you want me to email them to you?"

"We'll stop over this afternoon," I said. "Any drugs in Mosley's system?"

"Toxicology hasn't come back yet."

"Thanks, Tom. See you in a couple hours." I hung up.

"Drugs?" Lint asked.

"Toxicology isn't back yet."

"What's next?"

"Run a check on Doug Oliver's gun. Let's see when and where it was purchased. Then pull his financials and see if there was any life insurance on Jennifer Oliver."

"Roger that," said Lint. He began pounding away on his keyboard with his two stubby index fingers.

I got up and went for the coffee maker. "Coffee?" I asked.

"Yeah, thanks," Lint replied

I made us each a cup of coffee. We both drank it black. I set Lint's cup at the edge of his desk where I thought he might find it hardest to spill.

"Thanks," said Lint.

I returned to my desk and began reading through Jennifer Oliver's and Ron Mosley's personnel records. I blew in my coffee and sipped it as I read. It was true, Ron Mosley was an exemplary employee. He was liked by all of his coworkers and students as well. Mosley had never missed a day of work in his entire employment with North Myrtle Beach High School. Why did he suddenly start harassing a woman at work, and what could have made this man snap and stab that same woman to death in her own home? Could there be a cover-up? Could Jennifer Oliver have made the whole thing up? One thing was for certain: she was dead. She couldn't make that up.

Chapter Eight

By three o'clock that afternoon the story of Jennifer Oliver's murder was all over the news. And when we pulled up in front of Ronald Mosley's house, four news vans from four different TV stations were camped out front. Doug Oliver had already given his live interview from his brother's couch in Little River. Doug didn't leave anything out of the interview; he told everything. He told of the relentless sexual harassment of his wife, and even pontificated on the "big cover-up," as he phrased it. He even went so far as to blame the North Myrtle Beach school system for the murder of his wife.

Ron and Thelma Mosley lived at 4608 Woodland Street in a modest single-story, two bedroom home. The wooden board and batten siding was painted gray, and the aluminum trim was white. The paint job looked new, and so did the shingled roof. The home had no driveway, which kept most of the vulture like news reporters in the street.

When Lint and I climbed out of the Charger, the entire swarm descended on us with shouts of "Detective!

Detective!" The glassy eyes of the cameras spun our way in spooky unison.

"How's my hair?" Lint whispered.

"Greasy," I replied.

We made our way through the mob and onto the lawn.

"Detective!" one reporter called out. "Is this a hate crime?"

"Hate crime?" I asked.

"The victim was white," said the reporter.

"She was?" I shot back. "Wow, thanks for your help." We didn't answer any more questions even though they continued to shout them out. I heard something about a conspiracy and another one hollered something about women in the work place.

I knocked on the door, pressed the doorbell button, and reached for my shield. The door opened a crack, and a black woman I guesstimated to be in her late forties peered through the opening. I held my badge so she could see it and my face.

"I'm Detective Jake Stellar, and this is my partner, Detective Avis Lint. We were wondering if we could come in and ask you a few questions, Mrs. Mosley."

"Do you have a warrant?" asked the woman.

"Well, no," I replied. "We just wanted to ask you a few questions."

"First of all, I'm not Mrs. Mosley, I'm her sister. Second of all, you're not questioning Thelma without her lawyer present."

"Who is it?" we heard someone call out.

The woman turned and spoke to someone in another room. "It's the cops. They want to ask you a few questions. I told them not without your lawyer here."

"Let them in, Nadine,"

Glowering, Nadine pulled the door open. She didn't ask us in. We went in any way.

Thelma lay on the couch in her robe. Her eyes were swollen and bloodshot. Her hair was a mess. A glass of water sat on the coffee table next to her. "You'll have to excuse my sister," she said. "She's very protective of me, always has been."

I introduced Lint and myself. Thelma sat up and adjusted her robe. Even in her current state she was a very beautiful woman. "Please, sit," she said, motioning toward another matching sofa that sat against the front wall across from her.

Lint and I took seats on opposite ends of the couch. Nadine stood guard at the entrance to the room in a wide-legged bouncer's stance and her arms folded across her chest. She was giving us the squint-eyed, judgmental look that bible-thumping Aunt Esther used to reserve for heathenish Fred Sanford. I imagined Nadine might have once been as beautiful as her sister, but she now had that worn, wrinkled look of a woman who had spent too many hours in a bar, smoking too many cigarettes, and drinking way too much alcohol.

I began with the usual, "Sorry for your loss."

Thelma thanked me for that.

"Mrs. Mosley, your—"

"Please, call me Thelma," she said.

"Thelma, let me start by saying, your husband has no criminal history and there's nothing at all we can find in his past that would point to him committing a crime like this. We can't even find a parking ticket."

Thelma smiled. "Ron was a good man."

I looked over at Nadine to see her reaction, there wasn't one.

"Had there been any changes in his behavior in the days leading up to what happened?" Lint asked.

"No," Thelma replied. "Everything was fine." She looked over our heads out the picture window behind us. "He even bought me flowers last week." Her eyes went to a vase holding a dozen red roses on the end table to her left.

"Those?" I asked, knowing full well they were. I stood and walked to the vase. A floral pick card holder held a small envelope. "May I?" I asked.

Thelma nodded her head yes. I pulled the envelope from the holder and removed the card. The card said: I'M THE LUCKIEST MAN IN THE WORLD. LOVE, RON. I put the card back in the envelope and placed it back in the plastic holder. "Very nice," I said. I don't know why I said very nice. As far as I knew, Ron Mosley was a vicious rapist and murderer. He may have been the luckiest man in the world the day he sent those flowers, but last night his luck ran out.

We sat in Thelma Mosley's living room for another forty minutes asking questions. Thelma seemed to like to talk about Ron. She seemed to really care about him. Her eyes grew misty a few times during our interview, but she never broke down and cried. I had interviewed widows in the past, and this was very strange to me. Maybe Thelma was just stronger than most.

After we finished our questions, Nadine walked us to the door. I thanked her, but she didn't reply. It was obvious that Nadine hated cops. I didn't care; there was something about Nadine I didn't like either.

The vultures shouted out more questions as we walked back to the car. I ignored them. Lint asked, "Don't you people have anything better to do?" They didn't have anything better to do; being parasites was their job.

"What did the card say?" Lint asked.

I pulled the driver's side door shut. "I'm the luckiest man in the world ... Love, Ron."

"I wonder who holds that title now." Lint asked.

"Whoever was the second luckiest man on Monday," I replied. I put the Charger in drive and headed south.

"One of the girls—Becky, I think—got me a coffee mug one time that said World's Greatest Dad."

"Oh yeah?" I said.

"At the time I wondered if she really thought that."

"She probably did," I replied. "Kids are stupid."

"Hey!"

"Not just yours, all kids."

Lint chuckled. "Oh, that's better."

Avis Lint had eight children from three different marriages; he was still paying child support on three of the children, and alimony to one of the exes. From the stories he had told me over the past two years, I knew he wasn't the world's greatest father. There was a time when that didn't bother Lint, but as he got older, regret had begun to rear its ugly head.

I turned right onto Forty-Eighth Avenue. When we passed Hamburger Joe's, Lint said, "You ever eat there?"

"Had lunch there a few times," I responded.

"I could really go for one of Joe's cheeseburgers."

"We just ate lunch a little over two hours ago."

"I didn't mean right now."

"Sure you didn't."

Lint turned his head to the left. "Nacho Hippo's," he announced. "Their tacos are so—"

"Holy shit! You got a problem."

"Yeah, my problem is that there's too goddamn many restaurants in this town."

"There's too many golf courses in this town as well. Why don't you switch from eating to golfing?"

"I suck at golf, but I'm awesome at eating."

"I guess you got a point there."

"The lobster tacos are the best."

Chapter Nine

It was a thirty-minute drive over to the Horry County Coroner's Office in Conway. When we arrived Tom Powers was just finishing up for the day. We went directly to the examining room where we were told he was working. I pushed open the swinging double doors like a cowboy just coming off the range.

"Set 'em up, bartender," I said. After I said it, I wondered why I said it. I hadn't had a sip of alcohol in over fourteen years. Just saying the words *set 'em up, bartender* made me want a big glass of Scotch. It's funny how that works. "Someday you won't even think about alcohol," a therapist once told me. He lied. Fourteen years later I still have dreams about alcohol. I guess what he meant was, one day when your dead you won't even think about alcohol.

"Just closing her up, Jake," said Tom. He laid the medical instruments he was using on Jennifer Oliver's abdomen and pulled the white sheet up over her breasts.

"Tell us what happened so we can wrap this case up," said Lint.

"How would I know what happened?" Tom said. "I wasn't there."

"Then guess," I told him.

Tom sneered at me.

"I was joking," I said.

"Obviously," Tom replied. "Toxicology showed no drugs in Mrs. Oliver's or Mr. Mosley's blood. However, both had consumed about 300 milliliters of red wine."

"Not enough to be drunk," Lint said.

"No," agreed Tom, "not enough to be drunk, but a woman Mrs. Oliver's size may have been a little tipsy." Tom folded the sheet back down just enough to reveal the stab wounds. "There are seventeen stab wounds to Mrs. Oliver's torso. Many of them were superficial, hesitant wounds. The one that killed her is right here." Tom pointed at one of the deeper wounds. "The knife entered here and severed the hepatic artery; she bled to death in seconds. If you notice, the wounds are horizontal. Most people hold a knife like this"—Tom picked up a scalpel and demonstrated—"which means that Mr. Mosley most likely stood at the edge of the bed while stabbing Mrs. Oliver. Also, the knife penetrated at a slight angle from the victim's left to her right, which means Mr. Mosley stood on the left side of the bed—like I am now—while inflicting the wounds."

"Doug Oliver said Mosley was straddling his wife as he stabbed her," Lint pointed out.

"Well," said Powers, "That could very well be. He may have held the knife with the blade horizontal. It's just that most people don't."

"So, it's not enough to call him a liar," I surmised.

"Not at all," said Powers.

"Doc, what did you mean by hesitant wounds?" Lint asked.

"Most often hesitant wounds are self-inflicted. For example, when someone wants to commit suicide, but is just too afraid to go through with it. They will cut themselves, but not quite deep enough to cause any real damage."

"Are you saying some of Mrs. Oliver's wounds were self-inflicted?" I asked.

"Definitely not," Tom said. "I believe that Mr. Mosley just wasn't sure he wanted to go through with it at first. But when things got out of hand, he felt it was his only option."

"So you're positive that Mrs. Oliver's wounds came from Mr. Mosley?" I asked.

"It certainly looks that way. Semen samples taken from Mrs. Oliver matched DNA from Mr. Mosley. Mr. Mosley's hands and legs were stained with her blood. I haven't seen the CSI report, but I suspect they found Mr. Mosley's fingerprints on the knife."

"Was she raped before the stabbing," Lint asked, "or after?"

"Definitely before," said Tom.

"And it was forced sexual contact?" I asked.

"Yes," Tom replied. "There were no vaginal lacerations. However, there were bite marks around Mrs. Oliver's nipples that drew blood, and there was bruising to the inside of her thighs. Both are consistent with forced intercourse." Tom walked over to a desk on the other side of the room and picked up two file folders. One tab said Ronald Mosley and the other said Jennifer Oliver. He handed me the Ronald Mosley file. "This one is all finished, but I have some more work to do on Mrs. Oliver's. You want to take what I have, or do you want me to send it over when I'm finished?"

I took Mosley's file. "You can send Mrs. Oliver's over when you're finished," I said. "What time do you think that will be?"

Tom looked up at the clock over the door. "Sometime tomorrow morning," he replied. "I'm heading out in a few minutes."

We thanked Tom and headed back to North Myrtle Beach. When we arrived at the station, the CSI report was waiting for us. Tom was right: the fingerprints on the knife did match Ronald Mosley. Blood spatter on the walls and ceiling was consistent with Tom's description of what had taken place; Mosley stood on the left side of the bed while stabbing Mrs. Oliver. The three slugs they pulled out of Mosley and the one they pulled out of the wall matched Doug Oliver's pistol.

Records showed that Doug Oliver had purchased his revolver four days before the incident. A coincidence? Maybe.

I sat at my desk reading through Ronald Mosley's autopsy report. One bullet hit his liver, another hit his aorta, and the third came to rest in his left ventricle. Perfect shooting. Justified shooting. I closed the folder and straightened up my desk a little. I looked over at Lint. He was reading something on his monitor.

"I'm going to take off," I said.

Lint glanced up at the clock. It was ten minutes after five. "Yeah, me too," he said.

I stood and retrieved my weapon from the top drawer of my desk, and headed for the door. Gwen Lawrence and her partner Dill Perkins were coming in as I got to the door.

"Any word on the white mystery van?" I asked.

"Nothing yet," Perkins replied. "But I heard you and Lint harassed a poor old deaf guy." He and Gwen chuckled.

"He wasn't old," I protested, "just deaf. And it was Lint who made fun of him."

"What did I do?" Lint asked as he walked up behind me.

"Picked on that deaf guy yesterday," I replied.

Lint pushed on by us. "Who gives a shit? The guy was being a dick." He walked out the door.

"The guy *was* being a jerk," I agreed.

"Lint or the deaf guy?" Perkins asked.

"Both, I guess." I walked out the door.

Chapter Ten

I couldn't wait to get home; it had been a long day. I hadn't spoken with Bree all day and I hoped that when I pulled in the driveway and went inside, the house would be filled with the wonderful aroma of something she had fixed for dinner. Those dreams were soon crushed as I rounded the corner and saw Aida Trentinni's Lexus parked in my driveway ... right next to Bree's car.

A lot of things bug me, but one thing that really grates my nutsack is when someone else is parked in my driveway. Who does this? I don't. If I go to anyone's house, I park in the street. Anyone comes to my house, where do they park? Right in my driveway.

I drove up the street remembering the good old days when I would have just drove on by if someone was in my driveway, and went to a bar for a couple of hours until the coast was clear. I would feel pretty foolish these days sitting at a bar sipping a ginger ale. I made a U-turn and parked in the street in front of the house.

Aida Trentinni is Bree's best friend. She's a very nice woman and very attractive. The only problem with Aida is her husband, Luca. I can't stand Luca. He's everything I hate about a man all rolled up into one irritating bundle. He's a wealthy banker. He spends a lot of time at the gym. He's a black belt in karate … or judo … or some other bullshit. Luca once told me he could show me a few moves that might help me out in my line of work. At the time I thought about challenging him to a fight and then pulling out my gun and shooting him as he came at me.

As I walked up my driveway I prayed to God that Luca wasn't with Aida. I also thought about dragging my truck key down the side of her Lexus just to show her she shouldn't have been parked in my driveway.

When I walked into the dining room, Woofie ran right to me. "Hey, dog," I said.

Woofie danced in a circle and yipped.

"What's the matter, girl?" I asked. "Are you trying to tell me something? Is there an annoying bodybuilding karate-banker in the living room?"

Woofie let out a loud bark. I hoped that wasn't a yes.

An open, half-empty bottle of moscato sat on the kitchen table.

"Jake!" Bree hollered. "We're in here."

Thank God, I thought. *I never would have found them in this giant mansion of ours*. When I got to the living room I saw that my prayers had been answered. Luca was nowhere in sight.

"Where's Luca?" I asked.

"He had to work late," Aida replied. She tipped up her wine glass and downed the last of her moscato.

"Oh, that's too bad," I said.

Bree shot me a look. I wondered if my sarcasm was too blatant.

"What are you ladies up to this evening?" I asked.

"We just got back from the mall a few minutes before you got here," Bree answered.

"Good," I said. "I was just thinking the other day that you needed a bunch of new clothes."

Aida giggled.

"Watch it, smart-ass," said Bree.

"What's for dinner?" I asked.

"We were going to go to dinner with Aida and Luca," Bree replied, "but Luca's meeting is at seven."

"Oh that's too bad," I said, and then realized I had already used that line.

Bree glared at me. I don't know why it angered her so much. She knows how much I can't stand Luca. If she didn't want my sarcasm, then she shouldn't put me in a situations that calls for it.

Aida stood. "I better get going," she announced. She carried her wine glass to the kitchen and placed it in the sink. Bree got up from my recliner and followed her to the door. I reclaimed my recliner and turned the TV to The Weather Channel. Yup, it was just as I suspected, there was weather.

"Tell Luca I said hi!" I shouted.

"I will!" Aida hollered back.

Ha, she fell for it.

Bree refilled her wine glass on her way back to the living room and took a seat on the couch.

"Dodged that bullet," I said.

"I can't imagine what your problem is with Luca," said Bree.

"He's a douche," I said, never taking my eyes off the Doppler radar.

"What makes him a douche?"

"How about if I list the things that don't make him a douche. That list is a lot shorter."

"Funny."

"Yeah, I know, right?" I agreed. "I was just telling Lint today that I was funny."

"Why would you be telling him that?"

"Because he brought up the fact that he was the class clown when he was in school."

"I can see that," Bree said, nodding her head. "He seems like a Chris Farley/John Candy type of guy."

That caused me to look away from the Local on the 8s segment. "What?" If I had been drinking a ginger ale it would have been a spit take. "Chris Farley ... John Candy? How the hell could you compare Lint with either of those comedic geniuses?"

"Well, I mean, when he was a kid he was probably over-weight and probably had a little better sense of humor before three or four divorces and alimony and child support. He's funny now, so he was probably even funnier back then."

I rolled my eyes. "He's funny now?"

"He makes me laugh all the time."

"Me too, but I'm laughing at him, not with him."

"You're just mean, Jake."

"But funny mean, right?"

Bree stared at me for a second but didn't answer. I imagined a thought bubble forming over her head that said, "If you have to ask somebody if you're funny, you're probably not as funny as you think you are." Finally her head turned toward the TV. "Just put it back on the movie I was watching."

"What station was it?"

"Lifetime."

"Of course it was." I sat there with our conversation stewing in my head. "Who do you think is funnier, Lint or—"

Shhh!

"I just want to know—"

Shhh!

"This isn't over." I got up and went in to take a shower.

Chapter Eleven

Wednesday morning I was sitting at my desk in the squad room going over the Oliver files. I was leaning back in my chair with my feet up on my desk. I only did this if Merle wasn't in the building.

Lint was at his desk staring at his monitor; he was going over the Olivers' and Mosleys' financials.

"Nothing odd about these bank statements," Lint said. "But Doug Oliver purchased a life insurance policy on his wife a little over a year ago."

I looked up from the files. "How much?" I asked.

"A quarter of a million."

"A little over a year ago doesn't sound suspicious. What about the phone records?"

"Yeah, they came in last night." Lint hit a couple keys on the keyboard and turned the monitor so I could see.

I got up from my desk and walked over to Lint's desk. I leaned over and rested my palms on the top of his desk.

There was a call from Jennifer Oliver's cell phone to her husband's cell phone at 8:53 pm on the night of her murder; Doug Oliver was still at work at that time, probably getting ready to leave. Right before the call she placed to Doug there was a call to another number—a cell phone. As we read through Jennifer's call log we found eleven calls to that same number during the two weeks leading up to her death, and seven calls from that number to hers. Jennifer's cell phone records showed no text messages to that number, and the cell number didn't match the number of anyone involved in the case. After a search, we determined that it was a burner phone purchased three weeks ago for cash at a Walgreen's on North Kings Highway in North Myrtle Beach.

"I wonder if Walgreen's still has their surveillance footage from then?" Lint asked.

"Let's find out," I replied. I went back to my desk, retrieved my 9mm, and grabbed my sport coat that was hanging over the back of my chair.

Lint got up from his desk and slipped on his sport coat. "Hamburger Joe's?" Lint asked.

"It's only ten thirty, for Chrissakes."

"I mean after we go to Walgreen's."

We were almost to the door when Officer Pat Murray stuck his head into the squad room. "Jake," he said.

"I turned around. "Yeah, Pat, what is it?"

"Doug Oliver is here to see you."

"Oh yeah? Send him in." Lint and I walked back to the middle of the room.

Doug Oliver walked through the door holding a small, pink, hardcover book decorated with a floral motif. "Detectives," he said.

"Mr. Oliver," Lint replied. "What's up?"

He held the book out to Lint. "I was going through some of my wife's things this morning and I came across Jennifer's diary. I found it in a dresser drawer. I didn't even know she kept a diary."

He held the book out to Lint. He glanced at the cover, upon which Diary was embossed in a whimsical font, and passed it to me. I immediately noted the diary's cheap metal lock had been jimmied and no longer functioned.

"You forced the lock open, I see," I commented.

"Yes, I had to. I couldn't find the key."

"So you've already read it?" said Lint.

"Of course," Doug replied. "And you guys better read it too. Everything is in there."

"Everything, like what?" I asked. I opened the book and began flipping through the pages.

"About the sexual harassment," Doug replied. "It has names and dates. She documented everything from her first encounter with Mosley, until the night before she was … she was—"

"Thanks for bringing this in," I interrupted.

"Do you think it will help your investigation?"

"It should help answer a lot of questions," said Lint.

Doug looked from Lint to the book, and then back at me. "Okay, good."

"We'll be in touch, Mr. Oliver," Lint said.

Doug thanked us and took his leave.

Lint opened the diary and skimmed through its contents' "This should tell us everything we want to know, he remarked."

"Looks like," I agreed. I took the book from him and placed it in the top drawer of my desk. "Let's get over to Walgreen's."

"And then Hamburger Joe's," Lint added.

"Yes, dammit, then Hamburger Joe's."

As we headed for the door, Pat Murray stuck his head in the room again. "Jake?"

"What!"

"Just got a 911 call," said Pat, "about a suspicious white van."

"Where?" Lint asked.

"Creekside Mobile Home Park."

"Call Perkins and Lawrence," I said.

"Already did," said Pat. "They're en route. Perkins said to meet them at the park entrance at the corner of Little River Neck Road and Seagull Boulevard."

"Tell them we're on our way," I said.

"Roger that," said Pat.

Chapter Twelve

We rolled up to the entrance of Creekside Mobile Home Park with our siren silent and our light bar turned off. Detectives Dill Perkins and Gwen Lawrence stood outside their unmarked Crown Victoria. I pulled the Charger off the side of the road and parked in front of them.

Lint and I joined them at the edge of the street. "What do we have?" I asked.

"911 call came in about twenty minutes ago," said Perkins. "The caller said there's been a suspicious white van parked in his neighbor's driveway for three day."

"You think it's the same one you've been looking for?" I asked.

"Looks that way," said Perkins.

"There's a couple extension cords running from the trailer to the van," Gwen added.

"And the caller said even though his neighbor's car is also in the driveway, she hasn't seen the guy in a few days," Perkins explained. "In her words, 'something funny's going on,' and she figured it was high time the police got involved."

"The neighbor have a name?" I asked.

Gwen pulled a note pad from her back pocket and flipped through a couple pages. "Roy Carpenter," she said.

"Any activity around the van?" I asked.

"The caller said there have been two men she doesn't know staying at the trailer," said Gwen, "and she's seen them both walking back and forth to the van, sometimes staying inside for over an hour."

"Thank God for nosy neighbors," Lint commented.

"The neighbor has witnessed both men wearing what she called surgical masks," Perkins offered.

"Sounds like a mobile meth lab to me," said Lint.

"How do you want to do this?" I asked.

"Should we call SWAT?" asked Gwen.

Lint sneered. "SWAT? Why? We can do this. Break a window, throw in a flash grenade. *Bam!* We got 'em."

"More like, *boom!* Giant explosion," Perkins argued. "We can't throw a flash grenade into that van. That shit's highly flammable."

"He's right," I agreed. "We have to wait until they're both out of the van."

"That could take all day," Lint complained. "I'm getting hungry."

We ignored him.

"We don't know if the homeowner is inside the trailer," Gwen noted. "We'll have to take them outside, before they get to the trailer."

Gwen's voice was shaky as she spoke. I looked down at her hands; they were trembling. I glanced up at Lint, then Perkins. I wondered if either one of them noticed. They didn't seem to.

The mobile home we were watching sat at the south west corner of the park; on Sandpiper Street. To its east was another mobile home. To its south was House Creek, and to the west was a row of trees that stood in front of a six-foot wooden fence. The wooden fence surrounded a luxury retirement community. I imagined the well-heeled residents referred to themselves as *us*, and those in the mobile home park as *them*.

"How do you want this to go down, Gwen?" I asked.

"Uh … um. Why don't we—" She paused. "What do you think, Jake?"

I took out my cell phone and pulled up Google Maps. "Gwen, you're with me," I said. Lint and Perkins both gave me a strange look. I ignored it. I pointed at the trailer across the street from the one we were watching. "Lint, I want you at the back door of this place. Get anyone inside, out of the home. I want you camped out on the front porch; look like you belong there. It shouldn't be too tough for you to look like you belong in a trailer park."

"Roger that, Ja—hey!"

Perkins and Gwen chuckled.

I pointed at the trailer next door. "Perkins, you do the same with this place, then position yourself where you can see them, but they can't see you Gwen and I will enter the retirement community next door and watch from behind the fence. Everyone be at the ready. Perkins, you'll have the best view; we go on your call. Everyone keep your eyes open. Any questions?"

Everyone shook their heads and said, "No."

Lint and Perkins got in the Crown Vic and Gwen and I climbed into the Charger. We both started our cars. I nodded to Perkins, and we both headed for our stations.

Perkins parked his car on Osprey Street, one street over, and went the rest of the way on foot.

I took a left off of Little River Neck Road onto James Island Avenue and entered the retirement community. A Grecian-style arch festooned with Boston ivy straddled the entrance. I felt special just driving between the stone pillars. Rows of look-alike townhouses with manicured, postage stamp-sized lawns stretched toward the horizon. It was an idyllic place for snobbish, wealthy oldsters to enjoy their twilight years and contemplate death.

"Nice houses," Gwen commented, "you and me will never be able to afford joints like these. Not on our pitiful salaries."

I was reminded of a Dr. Seuss book my mother used to read me when I was a child. "Yup," I said. "These old farts have bellies with stars, and the trailer park folks have none upon thars."

Gwen chuckled in recognition of the tale. "*The Sneetches*," she said.

I looked over and smiled. When my smile faded I asked, "Are you okay?"

"Yes. Why?"

"I noticed your hands trembling a little bit back there. You looked nervous, like your mind was elsewhere."

"I'm fine."

I cocked my head and gave her the old *I don't really believe you* stare. "It's only been four months. It's okay to be scared."

Four months. That was how long it had been since Gwen was shot in the line of duty. We were outside a residence on Thirty-Fifth Avenue when a stray bullet hit her. She was wearing a vest at the time, but the round hit her in the hip, just below the vest. Gwen was a tough woman, one of the toughest I had ever met. Gwen's problem was that she always put up a brave front that made her look tougher than she really was. I knew she was nervous, and she was having a hard time trying to mask it. I didn't blame her; after all, getting shot isn't fun. In my opinion, she came back to work too early.

So far, there were only about twenty houses in the development. Judging by the amount of foundations that had been poured, many more townhouses were on their way. I pulled off the street and into a grassy vacant lot. I popped the trunk. We both got out and went around to the rear of the vehicle. I took off my jacket and tossed it into the trunk. I pulled out my tactical vest and put it on. Gwen did the same. Luckily the vests are adjustable, and she was able to wear Lint's vest. I went back around to the driver's side and grabbed a radio from its charger.

"Good?" I asked.

"I'm fine," Gwen acknowledged, none too convincingly. She adjusted the vest robotically.

We made our way to the wooden fence. The slats had shrunk up enough over time that we were able to get a good view of the trailer and the van parked in the driveway. There was no movement around the trailer, and there was no sign of Lint and Perkins yet. I grabbed the top of one of the slats and gave it a good yank. It came loose easier than I thought it would and it hit me right in the forehead. "Son of a bitch," I whispered.

Gwen laughed. "You want me to check the trunk for a hard hat?" she asked.

"No, smart-ass." I grabbed a second slat and pulled it off the fence. This gave Gwen and me a two-foot section to slip through when it was time. I crouched down and stared at the van. Gwen squatted down on the other side of the opening. I turned and looked behind me, taking in the entire retirement community. It seemed like a ghost town. The rich oldsters were probably all in the country club taking advantage of the early bird special, and putting down their "trailer trash" neighbors.

"Jake," came Perkin's voice from the radio, "I'm at the south west corner of the trailer next door. I'm just under the skirting. I have a clear view of the van and the front and rear door of the subject trailer."

"Roger that," I responded. "We go on your command."

"I'm on the front porch of the mobile home across the street, Jake," Lint reported. "The occupants have evacuated through the rear exit, and are staying with friends down the street."

"Roger that," I said into the mic. I peeked my head just inside the fence. Lint sat in a plastic lawn chair. He was leaning back on its two rear legs with his feet up on the railing. He had a beer bottle in his hand. He saw me looking and raised the bottle in a toast. I shook my head and hoped the rear legs of that chair could hold out under the fat bastard's load until the bust.

It was a good half hour before Gwen and I heard a trailer door slam.

"I have eyes on one of the perps," said Perkins. "He just left the trailer and is walking to the van." There was a short pause. "He's inside the van. Stand by."

I removed my weapon from my shoulder holster. Gwen pulled her weapon from the holster she had clipped to her waistband.

"The van door just opened again. The second perp has exited and is moving toward the trailer. He's inside."

"Dammit," I said.

We waited another half hour. It was time to make something happen. I picked up the radio. "Lint."

"Go ahead, Jake," said Lint.

"Why don't you go back inside and get another beer? Then walk across the street and see if your neighbor, Roy, wants to have a drink with you."

"Good idea," said Lint.

"Be careful."

"Don't worry," Lint joked, "I've had beers with neighbors before. It's not that dangerous."

"Get ready Perkins," I said.

"Roger that."

I turned to Gwen and said, "Come on." We slipped through the opening in the fence and duck walked through the row of pines to the back of the trailer. We put our backs against the skirting. I craned my neck around the corner to see Lint walking down the steps and across the street toward us. He saw me, but played it cool.

Lint walked along a dirt path and up the steps to the door. He pounded on the door a couple times and shouted, "Roy! You home?"

I pointed with my 9mm to the far end of the trailer. Gwen nodded and quickly as she could crawled in that direction. I watched until she disappeared around the corner.

"Hey, Roy!" Lint shouted again. "Answer the door, buddy! I got a brewski for ya!"

I turned and pulled at a loose piece of skirting, making an opening to climb through. I crawled under the trailer to the other side. There was no skirting under the front porch, so I rolled over onto my back and positioned myself right underneath Lint. I pulled out my weapon.

I heard the van door slide open; so did Lint. He turned around.

The deaf guy we had talked to on Monday stepped out of the van.

You son of a bitch, I thought.

"Wanoo you wan?" the guy asked Lint. "Hey! Inno you!" He stepped back, reached inside the van and pulled out a sawed-off shotgun. "Cops!"

"Gun!" Lint shouted. I heard both beer bottles hit the deck above me.

I rolled to my side and fired two rounds; one hit the van's tire, the other hit the perp in the shin. As the big deaf guy dropped I saw Lint's round hit him in the chest, knocking him back against the van's rocker panel. The deaf guy rolled to his side still clutching his weapon.

As beer rained down on me from above, I got to my knees and crawled out from under the porch.

Lint ran down the steps and met me at the moaning deaf guy.

"Drop it!" I ordered.

Lint kicked his shotgun away from him.

"How's that feel, Ferrigno?" Lint sneered.

"Funk you," said the big guy.

Lint dropped to his knees and hand cuffed him while I watched the windows and door of the trailer. I licked my lips. It was the first time I had tasted beer in a long, long time. It was really good.

I motioned for Perkins and Gwen to stay where they were and then helped Lint get the wounded man around to the other side of the van.

"Call it in," I said.

Lint got on his radio and called for backup and an ambulance.

I went back to the front of the van. "Police!" I shouted. "We have the trailer surrounded. Come out with your hands in the air!"

A jalousie window to the left of the front door opened. "I've got the homeowner in here! Stay back or I'll kill him."

"How do we know he's still alive?" I shouted back. I turned to Lint. "If he brings him to the door," I advised in an undertone, "shoot through the wall. The walls of these old trailers are pretty thin."

Lint nodded, turned, and went to the rear of the van. He brought up his revolver and trained it on the trailer.

I glanced back at Perkins; his weapon was on the trailer as well. I couldn't see Gwen from my position.

"I'm okay!" came a second voice from the trailer.

"Bring him to the door!" I hollered. "I want to see for myself."

"I'm not opening that door!"

"Bring him to the door, or we're coming in!" I shouted.

A few seconds later the door swung open. The homeowner stood in the doorway. The perp, who was standing just out of view behind the wall, had his revolver pressed against the homeowner's upper arm.

"You okay, Roy?" I asked.

"Y-yes," he replied.

"You the only one in there besides the gunman?" I asked.

He nodded crisply. I noticed his chin was quivering.

Just loud enough for Lint to hear me, I said, "Take the shot."

Lint fired his weapon three times into the wall just to the left of the door.

Roy flinched, and the gunman's weapon dropped to the floor. Perkins and I ran to the door with our weapons trained on the opening. "Get down!" I shouted.

Roy dropped to his knees with his hands in the air. When I got to him I could see the tears streaming down his face. "Praise Jesus!" Roy cried out, reaching his arms to the heavens. "Thank you, Jesus, thank you!"

The perp lay on the floor, his blood spilling onto Roy's avocado green shag carpet circa 1972. One of Lint's rounds had come to rest in his shoulder, and the other found a home in the scumbag's temple. The third round was probably somewhere in Roy's living room wall— lodged in a black velvet portrait of Jesus, no doubt.

Perkins helped Roy to his feet and out the door.

I walked to the end of the trailer to find Gwen sitting with her back to a propane tank and her knees pulled up to her chest. She held her weapon in her hand, with her other arm wrapped around her knees. She stared straight out over House Creek.

Gwen had told me she was all right, and she may have even believed it herself. But now we both knew that wasn't true.

Chapter Thirteen

A few hours later Gwen rode back to the station with me; Lint rode back with Perkins.

"Things are pretty slow right now," I said. "When we get back to the station, you're going to go into Merle's office and tell him you need a couple weeks off."

"But Jake—"

"I'm not asking you, I'm telling you."

Gwen slumped down in her seat and stared out the passenger side window. She looked like a teenage girl who had been told she couldn't go to the Taylor Swift concert.

"I want you to talk to someone," I said.

"I already talked to a shrink," Gwen replied.

"I'm not talking about the department shrink. I'm going to give you the number of I guy I used to talk to— still do every once in a while."

Gwen looked over at me, but I stared at the road ahead.

"This will stay between you and me," I said.

"And this guy you want me to spill my guts to," she said.

"He's good, Gwen. He got me through some rough times."

"Whatever. Maybe I just shouldn't be a cop anymore."

"I don't want to hear any of that bullshit. Have you said anything to Perkins about this?"

"Why would I say anything to Perkins?" she asked.

"Gwen, everyone at the department knows you two have been seeing each other for over a year now."

She looked over at me, utterly shocked. I wondered how she thought she and Perkins could keep this a secret from a building full of cops.

"Does Merle know?" she asked.

"He was one of the first to figure it out."

"That's just great."

"No one's going to say anything, as long as it doesn't affect your performance."

"I don't think my performance could get any worse at this point."

"So, what have you said to him?"

"Nothing. He keeps asking if I'm okay and I keep telling him I am."

We pulled into the parking lot of the North Myrtle Beach Police Department and climbed out of the car. Perkin's steered the Crown Vic into a spot right next to us.

"Everything okay?" Perkins asked.

Gwen gave me a *see what I mean* look. "Everything is fine," she said.

"All good," I agreed.

When we got inside, I went for the coffee pot, and Gwen went directly to Merle's door. She knocked a couple times and went in. She closed the door behind her.

Lint walked up next to me at the coffee stand. "What's going on?" he asked.

"We'll talk about it later." That was my way of quickly shutting him up. I had no intention of discussing it later—at least not the whole truth.

As I poured old, grayish green coffee into my cup, the low sound of distant rolling thunder came from Lint's body. "What the hell was that?" I asked.

"My stomach," Lint replied. "I'm starving."

I glanced up at the clock; it was a little after five. "Let's go get something to eat," I suggested, "and then we'll head over to Walgreens."

"Great idea," Lint responded.

I brought the mug up to my nose and sniffed. "I bet that's nasty." I set the cup back on the table and walked away. "Come on," I said.

As I went out the exit to the parking lot, I looked back over my shoulder at Merle's office door. Gwen was still in there. I hoped I had made the right decision.

Lint and I got in the Charger and headed south on North Kings Highway.

"So, what was going on with Gwen?" Lint asked.

"She wanted to take a couple weeks off to go see her parents," I said.

"Why'd she talk to you about it?"

"She just asked how I thought Merle would take it, since she had just came back to work a few weeks ago."

"Things have been slow," said Lint. "He shouldn't care."

"That's what I told her."

"Everything okay with her folks?"

"I guess."

"Seems odd she'd ask for vacation time at such a short notice."

"Not really."

"You think one of them is sick?"

"How would I know?"

"She didn't say why she had to see them now?"

"No."

"Strange. Should we ask her?"

"No."

"Well, I mean if one of them—"

"What are you getting," I asked, just trying to shut him up, "a cheeseburger?"

"Probably."

Lint got a faraway look in his eye. His mind had switched channels from Gwen's parents to cheeseburgers. I figured that would work.

"Maybe I'll get a cheeseburger all the way," Lint said, putting way too much emphasis on "all the way." However, he did make "all the way" sound very tasty.

At Hamburger Joe's, all the way meant your burger was topped with coleslaw, chili, and onions.

"Yeah," I said, "I'll probably get mine all the way too."

"Great minds," Lint commented.

Chapter Fourteen

Wheel of Fortune was half over when I finally walked in the door. Bree was curled up on the couch with a small blanket over her legs and a glass of moscato on the end table next to her. Woofie lay snuggled up on the blanket next to her legs. The slider was open to the back patio.

"What's going on?" I asked.

Bree put up a wait-a-minute finger and didn't take her eyes off the television screen.

A man in his dress blues said, "I'd like to buy a T please, Pat."

Vanna walked in front of the letters as three of them illuminated. She tapped them and the Ts appeared.

"A cut above the rest is history!" Bree shouted. "Yes!" She held out a hand to hive-five me. I gave it to her.

"Nice job," I said. I meant it. *Wheel* was a show that had always baffled me. My mind just didn't work that way. I don't know why. I can't explain it. I can sit there and watch as letter after letter is turned over, and nothing will come to mind. My only input when Bree and I watch is saying, "Oh, yeah," when someone else gets it. Oh well, who cares? I'm still pretty good at *Jeopardy*.

I walked back into the kitchen and placed my 9mm into the cupboard over the microwave, and took off my holster. I wound the strap around the holster and laid it in the cupboard next to my weapon.

"There's some lasagna in the fridge," Bree called out.

"Awesome," I said, and went to take a shower.

I returned to the living room a little while later wearing a white T-shirt, my blue and yellow board shorts, and my house shoes. Bree had reheated the lasagna for me. It was sitting on the end table next to my recliner, along with a glass of ginger ale. I sat down and dug in.

Woofie sat on the floor at my feet the entire time I ate, just staring at me. What a loyal friend he is when I have food on my lap. I picked a piece of hamburger meat out from in between the noodles and dropped it on the floor.

"Don't feed that to her," Bree said.

"It's hamburger meat," I pointed out.

"With sauce on it," Bree said.

I dropped another piece next to her and she gobbled it up. "She seems to like it."

Bree just shook her head.

Wheel of Fortune ended, and I asked Bree to put it on The Weather Channel for a second. The Local on the 8s segment ended just as I looked up from my plate. *Ugh*, I thought. *Another ten minutes*.

"How was your day?" Bree asked.

"Long," I replied.

"How's the thing with the teacher going?" she asked.

"It's going," I remarked.

Bree could usually tell when I didn't want to discuss work. It was usually when I got home after seven. She didn't ask about work again. I really appreciated that.

I finished my lasagna, sat my empty plate on the end table, and the local weather came up on the screen along with the usual elevator music.

It was currently seventy-three degrees and sunny. It was supposed to be sunny tomorrow with a high of seventy-six. It was also supposed to be sunny the day after that, but temperatures were expected to dip into the high sixties.

Three sunny days in a row, I thought. *That's why we moved to North Myrtle Beach.* I bet you could count on one hand the number of times there had been three sunny days in a row in the Bronx in the last hundred years. Even after twelve or thirteen years on the Grand Strand, I still appreciated the beautiful weather. I usually only missed the snow one day a year, and that was Christmas. I guess I fixated on The Weather Channel because the forecasts confirmed what I already knew: Bree and I were lucky to be living in paradise'

Bree got up and left the room, with Woofie right behind her. I switched the station over to *Jeopardy*. Alex had left his podium and was speaking with the contestants.

"What's this book on the table?" Bree asked, from the kitchen.

"Oh, yeah," I answered. "Can you bring that in here?"

Bree entered the living room holding Jennifer Oliver's diary. "Whose diary?" she asked.

"The deceased. Jennifer Oliver."

Bree handed me the diary. "The woman who was stabbed?"

"Yeah."

"Hold old was she?"

"Forty-four."

"And she kept a diary?"

"Yeah. Why, is that strange?"

"Well, I mean, most women keep a diary at some point in their lives—I kept one myself as a teenager—but still, at forty-four?"

"I always hear about women keeping journals," I argued.

"Yeah," Bree said, pointing at the diary, "but that's a diary like you would buy at Walmart as an impulse purchase for a teenage girl. Seems to me a woman documenting her sexual harassment would record her private thoughts in something more reserved and dignified—in case that documentation were ever revealed in court. This diary makes her claims seem frivolous."

"I didn't know you knew so much about diaries."

"I didn't know you knew so little." Bree picked my dinner plate up off the end table and took it into the kitchen. Woofie's toenails pitter-pattered across the tile as she tagged along.

"I'm taking the dog for a walk," Bree said.

"Yup," I replied.

I started with page one in the diary and began reading. *Today is the first day of summer*, it started off. I sat there for an hour, or so, reading page after page. At first Ronald Mosley was mentioned about once a week, but as time went on, he was mentioned more frequently. Jennifer seemed to enjoy Ronald's attention, and even harmlessly joked back and forth with him, but as things escalated, she tried to let him know tactfully she was happily married and wasn't interested in him romantically. According to Jennifer's diary, she continued to ask him to stop his overtures, but the attention he paid her soon turned into harassment. Jennifer described how she went to the principal with complaints, and was told over and over again that Ronald would be spoken to, but the harassment continued. She talked about finally going to the superintendent of the school district. Three weeks after speaking with the superintendent, Jennifer was let go.

The last entry in the diary was two days before Jennifer was murdered. On that day she describes being frightened, because Ronald kept driving by the house. She expressed wanting to phone the police, but her husband, Doug, told her not to. According to the diary, Doug told Jennifer that Ronald would eventually get bored and turn his attention to someone else.

When I finished reading, I flipped back through the pages, in order to confirm the handwriting was the same; it appeared to be. Some pages were written in blue ink, some were written in black ink, and some were written in pencil.

I closed the diary and put it on the end table. "Is there any more of that lasagna?" I hollered.

There was no answer.

"Hey!" I shouted. "Was that it for the lasagna?"

Nothing.

What the hell?

I pulled myself out of my recliner and went in search of Bree. I checked the bedroom, the bathroom, her closet, and the garage. I hit the button to open the garage door and walked outside. I walked around the side of the house and peeked over the fence into the backyard. *Where the hell did she go?*

I walked back to the driveway and stood there. I looked up and down Twenty-Fifth Avenue. I walked to the corner and looked up Hillside Drive. Bree was walking the dog toward me.

I waited until she got to me and asked, "Why didn't you tell me you were leaving?"

"I told you I was taking the dog for a walk," she replied.

"You did?"

"Yeah."

"I probably didn't hear you."

"You said, 'yup,' when I told you."

"Oh."

"You never listen to me."

We walked back to the house together.

"Why were you looking for me, anyway?" Bree asked. "Did you think I was abducted?"

"No. I was wondering if that was it for the lasagna," I said.

Bree stopped in her tracks. "Instead of just looking in the fridge for the lasagna, you searched the entire house and neighborhood for me?"

"I didn't search the *entire* neighborhood."

"How long did it take you to find me?"

"I don't know."

"You probably could have gotten out the lasagna and put a piece in the microwave, and even eaten it in the time it took you to find me."

I turned and started walking again. "Well, next time let me know when you're leaving."

"I did!"

Chapter Fifteen

I got to work at nine on Thursday morning. Lint was already at his desk drinking coffee, cramming Krispy Kremes into his pork trap, and grinning like an idiot into his cell phone screen. *I don't know, maybe I'm too critical of the big guy.*

"What are you looking at?" I asked, trying to sound interested, and a little less critical.

"A text from Bertie," said Lint. "She calls me her big teddy muffin."

I couldn't even fake a smile. To me, "big teddy muffin" sounded like a bear turd. I was just glad I hadn't eaten yet. "Hey, that's what I was going to start calling you," I said.

"*Partner* is fine."

"Let's take it slow."

"The security footage is in from Walgreen's" Lint informed me.

"Nice."

"It's already loaded into your computer."

"Who did that?"

"I did."

"Thanks." I sat down at my desk and pulled up the file named "Walgreens security footage." *How original*, I thought. The footage was four viewpoints, each taking up a quarter of the screen. One camera showed the entrance door. Another camera showed the parking lot. One was aimed down the aisle with cell phones, and the final camera was pointed at the checkout counter.

Lint got up from his desk and stood next to me.

"You see this yet?" I asked.

"No, I hate watching movies alone. Walgreen's records show the phone was purchased at 11:38 a.m."

I fast forwarded to eleven thirty and hit play. A minute later Doug Oliver walked through the door. He walked directly to the cell phones, looked at them for a while, and pulled one from the rack. He walked up to the cash register, and paid cash for the phone.

"I guess we better ask Doug Oliver if he knows anything about that cell phone," said Lint.

"Looks like," I agreed. "You have the address in Little River where he's staying?"

"Yeah, it's on my desk." Lint turned and shuffled some papers around on his desk. "Here it is."

We met Captain Stein halfway across the parking lot. "Where we at on the Oliver thing?" he asked.

"We traced a burner phone back to Doug Oliver," I replied. "We're headed over to Little River to speak to him about it."

"What's Perkins on?"

"He's got some paperwork to finish up this morning on the mobile meth lab, and then I'm sending him to the Home Depot in Myrtle Beach to speak with Doug Oliver's coworkers."

"Keep me posted," said Merle, and continued on his way. He paused after a few feet and turned. "Oh yeah, and Gwen is taking a couple weeks off to go see her parents. I'm putting a uniform with Perkins until she gets back."

"Is everything okay with her folks?" Lint asked.

"She didn't say," Merle replied, and went inside.

Lint and I turned around and headed for the Charger.

"I should have taken the captain's exam," Lint commented.

"Why's that?" I asked.

"It'd be nice to wear a white shirt every day and do nothing but ask, 'How's this thing going,' and 'How's that thing going?'"

"I think the cap'n does a little more than that."

"Very little," Lint grumbled.

I found it funny that we had come to a day in which Avis Lint was commenting on how little someone else worked. Before he became my partner, he was the laziest cop in the precinct. For all of Lint's faults, I have to say, he's come a long way in the last couple of years. I think some might even call him a good cop. Not me of course, but some.

Chapter Sixteen

Doug Oliver's brother, Dennis, lives on Queens Road in Little River, just outside the North Myrtle Beach city limits. We pulled into the driveway of the white vinyl-sided ranch, and I shut off the engine.

"How long you think before you could go back in your house if Bree was murdered there?" Lint asked, as we walked up the sidewalk to the front door.

"Could you possibly ask a more foolish or disturbing question?" I responded.

"I'm sure I can," said Lint.

I knocked on the door, pressed the doorbell button, and reached for my badge. Lint reached for his badge as well.

A short, thin brunette, probably on the sunny side of forty, pulled the door open.

"I'm Detective Jake Stellar, and this is my partner, Detective Avis Lint. We're with the North Myrtle Beach Police department. We'd like to speak with Doug Oliver."

"Certainly," the woman said. "I'm Doug's sister-in-law, Martha Oliver. Please come in."

We stepped into the living room and Martha closed the door behind us.

"Thank you," I said, and put my badge away.

"Can I get you gentlemen a cup of coffee? I just made a fresh pot."

"No, thank you," I said.

"That would be great," said Lint. "Thank you."

"Right this way," said Martha. We followed her down a hallway to the combination kitchen and dining room. "Please have a seat." She motioned toward the round table with a whitewashed finish on her way to a matching cupboard. "It's just terrible, what happened," she remarked as she selected two mugs.

"Excuse me?" I said.

Martha filled the mugs with coffee. "Jennifer's murder," she said. "Just terrible."

"Yes, it is," I said.

Lint was eyeballing a sheet cake with chocolate frosting that was sitting on the counter top a foot away from the coffee maker.

"The two of them had put everything in the past, and were really starting to work on their marriage," Martha commented.

Lint and I gave each other a look.

"Put everything in the past?" Lint asked.

Martha brought the coffee to the table. "Maybe I shouldn't say anything," she said. "You know—don't speak ill of the dead, and all that."

"What type of problems were they having, Mrs. Oliver?" I asked.

Martha got a strange look on her face when I questioned her. It was obvious she suddenly realized she may have said too much. She looked a little nervous, like a child who had inadvertently admitted to wrongdoing. "I, uh ... they just," she stuttered. "Nothing, really."

"If there's something you want to tell us," Lint said, "please do."

"What problems, Mrs. Oliver?" I asked.

I noticed Martha's hands were beginning to tremble.

"Good morning, Detectives," said Doug Oliver from the hallway. "What brings you to Little River?"

Martha's shoulders tensed. "They wanted to speak with you," she said.

Doug stepped into the room and glanced down at the two mugs of coffee Martha had poured. Martha picked up one of the mugs and placed it front of Lint. Doug picked up the other and started to put it in front of me.

I put up my hand. "No thanks," I said. "Just had a cup at the station."

Doug lifted the cup to his lips and blew. "Thank you, Martha," he said. "I'll take it from here."

Without another word, Martha turned and walked back down the hall.

Doug sat down to my right, across from Lint. "So, what can I do for you gentlemen?" he asked. He took a sip of his coffee.

"Your wife's cell phone records show her making several calls to a burner phone in the two weeks leading up to her death," I stated.

Doug cocked his head. "A burner phone?" he asked. "What's that?"

"A pre-paid cell phone," said Lint.

"Oh, oh, yeah," said Doug, nodding his head. "*That* cell phone. Okay, yeah, that was mine. I bought that … at Walgreen's, I think."

"Was there any particular reason you needed two cell phones, Doug?" Lint asked.

"My other cell phone kept messing up, so I bought that one to use."

"Why didn't you get yours fixed?" Lint asked.

"Well," said Doug, "my contract is just about up—you can check with Verizon if you like—and I figured I would just use the pre-paid one until I got my new one."

"I see. Would you mind if we had a look at that cell phone?"

"The pre-paid one?" Doug asked.

"Yes."

"I don't know what happened to that phone. I must have lost it, or misplaced it somewhere."

"If you come across it, let us know," said Lint.

"I sure will."

"Martha said something about some trouble you and Jennifer had put behind you," Lint asked. "What was that about?"

"Trouble?" Doug said. "I wouldn't say it was trouble, really. I mean, we've had our share of—"

"Trouble," said Lint.

Doug grinned. "Arguments," he said. "We've had our share of arguments. You know what I mean. Are you married Detective?"

"Three times," said Lint proudly.

"So then you do know what I mean."

"What were these little arguments about?" I asked.

"Money, housework—you know, things like that."

"Your money problems should be taken care of now," Lint said.

"What do you mean by that?" asked Doug.

"The life insurance," Lint said.

"We both had a life insurance policy. You can check."

"We did," I said.

"Did you look through Jennifer's diary?" Doug asked.

"I did," I said.

"It pretty much says everything, doesn't it?"

"Pretty much," I agreed.

Doug took another sip of coffee. He started to get up from the table. "Is that everything then?"

"For now," I said. I looked over at Lint. His eyes were still on the cake.

"One more thing," Lint said.

"Yes, Detective?"

"Is that white cake with chocolate frosting?"

"I think it is. Martha made it yesterday."

Lint got up from the table and so did I.

"Would you like to take a piece with you?" Doug asked.

"If you insist," replied Lint.

Doug cut Lint a piece and put it on a paper plate, along with a plastic spork and a napkin, considerate guy that he was. We left without seeing Martha Oliver again. I wanted to question her more, but figured that should be at a time when Doug wasn't around. I backed the Charger out of the driveway and drove back down Queens Road.

I glanced over at Lint. "Where the hell did that piece of cake go?" I asked.

"I ate it."

"Already? We just got in the car."

"It was bite-size," he defended, licking his lips.

Maybe in Lint's opinion that piece of cake was bite-size, but to any normal human being, it was five or six forkfuls. I just shook my head.

"If you wanted a piece of cake, Jake, you should've just asked."

"I didn't want a piece."

"It was so good."

"I'm glad you enjoyed it." *Dammit! All I can think about is cake.*

Chapter Seventeen

We drove straight back to the station and I called Chavez, in IT, from my desk.

"Chavez." he answered.

"Hey, Chavez, it's Jake. I need a location on a lost cell phone."

"You have the number?"

"Yes." I gave him the number, and he said he would call back when he had something. He also reminded me that the only way he could locate it was if the battery was still in it. I knew if it wasn't, that someone had probably taken it out so it couldn't be found.

I thanked Chavez and hung up.

"You're thinking that cell phone got lost on purpose, aren't you?" Lint said from his desk.

"Yes."

"Me too. What was in that diary?"

"Everything," I said. "She didn't leave anything out."

"How helpful."

"Yeah. Bree says the diary looks like something a teenage girl would use, not a woman Jennifer Oliver's age."

"I know what she means," said Lint. "Bertie writes in a journal every day, but it's just one of those composition notebooks that she wrote JOURNAL on the front with a pen she keeps clipped to it."

"What do you mean, 'clipped to it'?"

"She has a rubber band wrapped around the notebook and she slides the pen in between the book and the band."

"So, she always uses the same pen?"

"Pretty much, I guess. Whenever I look over, she's got that same pen in her hand. Why?"

"In Jennifer's diary, there's no consistency in the way the entries are written. One day it's with a blue pen, the next it's with a black one. Sometimes the entries are in pencil."

Lint shrugged. "Could mean something," he said. "Or it could mean she didn't have a rubber band."

Perkins walked through the door.

"What did Doug's coworkers have to say about him?" I asked.

"Did they say he was a raging homicidal maniac?" Lint asked.

Perkins laughed. "No, nothing like that. Everyone pretty much described him as a regular guy."

"A regular guy," I repeated. "Ron Mosley's coworkers said he was a regular guy too."

"Someone's lying," said Lint.

"They didn't say he was perfect," Perkins added.

"What do you mean?" I asked.

"A few of his coworkers said that there was a rumor awhile back that he was seeing someone at the store. A cashier."

"You got this someone's name?" Lint asked.

"Sure do." Perkins reached into his shirt pocket and pulled out a slip of paper. "Oksana Alexandrova," he read. "A cute little twenty-four-year-old."

"Sounds like a Russian figure skater," said Lint.

Perkins laughed and handed me the paper. "Name, number, and address. She has today and tomorrow off."

"Thanks," I said. "Is that it?"

"One last thing."

"What is it?"

"Doug Oliver called Home Depot this morning and put in his two week notice, but since he had two weeks of vacation coming, he's all done as of today."

"A quarter of a million won't last him the rest of his life," Lint pointed out.

"Not in this country anyway," I said.

"Maybe he's moving with Oksana to Russia," Perkins joked.

"The money probably wouldn't last long there either," I said. "But we better go have a talk with Ms. Alexandrova."

"You need me for anything else?" asked Perkins.

"No," I replied.

"I'm going to lunch then." He turned and waked away.

"Perkins," I said.

He turned back. "Yeah?"

"Ron Mosley has a sister-in-law named Nadine. We didn't get her last name when we questioned the wife. See if you can get me a last name and contact information on her."

"You got it," said Perkins.

"You think we should also have Martha Oliver come in so we can talk to her alone?" Lint asked.

"I think we better."

The phone on my desk rang. "Stellar," I answered.

"It's a no-go on the cell phone," Chavez said. "And those calls from Jennifer Oliver's phone to the missing one, they could have been to anywhere in the city."

"That's what I figured. Thanks any way." I hung up.

"What is it?" Lint asked.

"Can't locate the burner," I said. I got out of my chair. "Come on."

I headed for the door and Lint followed.

"Did you see that?" Lint asked, when we got outside.

I looked up at the sun and pulled my sunglasses out of the inside breast pocket of my sport coat. "See what?" I asked.

"I made Perkins laugh twice in there."

"So?"

"You said I wasn't funny."

"You're not."

"I didn't see him laugh at anything you said."

I pulled open the driver's side door and got in. "I wasn't trying to make him laugh."

"Me neither. It just comes naturally when you're the class clown."

I laughed, and then caught myself.

"See what I mean?" said Lint

I started the engine and we stopped at the red light at the corner of North Kings Highway and Second Avenue.

"We're gonna eat first, right?" Lint asked.

"I guess," I replied. "Where do you want to eat?"

"I don't care, you decide."

"Just pick a place."

"Sonic."

"That's what I figured."

"You're grumpy today."

"No I'm not."

"Still mad about the cake?"

"I wasn't mad about the—just shut up."

Chapter Eighteen

Oksana Alexandrova lived in a small two bedroom ranch at the end of Weatherwood Drive, in a cul-de-sac.

"Pretty nice place for a cashier at Home Depot," Lint commented, on our way up the driveway to the front door. I took a closer look. It was a nice house on a Home Depot cashier salary. Hell, it was a nice house on my salary.

I knocked. She answered. I showed my badge, and made the usual introduction.

"What's this about?" were the first words out of her mouth, while standing half hidden behind the front door.

"May we come in, Ms. Alexandrova?" I asked. "Alexandrova"—that was an extremely cool name to say out loud. I felt like I was in a James Bond flick. Daniel Craig, eat your heart out.

"Do you have a warrant?" was her second question.

"You can let us in, or we can question you at the station," Lint said.

Oksana stepped back and pulled the door the rest of the way open. "Come in." She turned and walked into the living room. Lint and I followed her. I left the front door open.

Oksana was just over five feet tall with long, blonde, messy, hair that was in bad need of a retouch. If her skin was slightly darker one might not notice the dark circles under her eyes, but with her milky white complexion, they were very pronounced.

"I thought she would sound like Natasha Fatale," Lint whispered. "You know, Rocky and Bullwinkle?"

I ignored him.

When Oksana got to the middle of the room, she stopped and turned around. "What do you want?"

"We were wondering if we could ask you a few questions about, Doug Oliver." I said.

"Doug?" She tried to look surprised. She was a terrible actress. "Why? Are you asking everyone at work about him?"

"Why would we ask everyone?" Lint asked.

"Well, he's the manager and he—"

"You're the only one dating him," said Lint.

Oksana burst out laughing. "Dating him?"

"I may have been the class clown when I was a kid," Lint said, "but that wasn't meant as a joke." He shot me a look out of the corner of his eye.

What an asshole, I thought. "Several of your coworkers say the two of you are dating," I clarified.

"I don't know why they would say that," said Oksana.

"Because it's true," said Lint, as he walked over and picked up a framed 5"x7" photograph of the two of them that had been neatly arranged on a table in front of the picture window.

Oksana's pale cheeks flushed. "We're just friends," she said.

"Try again," I said.

"Am I going to need a lawyer?"

"Do you think you need a lawyer?" I asked.

"Doug Oliver's wife is dead," Lint stated, "there's a quarter of a million dollar life insurance policy, and you're Doug's girlfriend. Did you do something that makes you think you might need a lawyer?"

"No, I didn't do anything. It was that black man who did it. Ron somebody—he killed Doug's wife."

"Did Doug tell you that?" I asked.

"It was on the news," Oksana replied.

"But did Doug actually tell you Ron Mosley killed his wife?" Lint asked.

"Yes, he told me so."

"Well," said Lint, "I guess if Doug said it, it must be true."

"Are you being sarcastic?"

"Do you have to ask?"

"Listen, Ms. Alexandrova"— Loved saying that name—"if there's anything you think you should tell us, now is the time."

"There's nothing to tell you," she replied. "Doug and I have been seeing each other, it's true. We've been seeing each other for about three months, but Doug is a good man. He wouldn't have hurt his wife. Besides, everyone says it was the other man ... Mosley. They said on the news that he stabbed Mrs. Oliver and that Doug shot him and killed him."

"Did Doug ever tell you he was going to leave his wife?" I asked.

"Yes," Oksana replied. "He said he was going to divorce her and we were going to move to Costa Rica."

"Why Costa Rica?" Lint asked.

"That's where my parents live part of the year," said Oksana. "They have a house there, and a house in Spain. This house is also theirs."

"What does your father do?" Lint asked.

"He's in international real estate."

"So Doug was going to leave his wife and the two of you were going to live in Costa Rica," I said, just to make sure I had it right.

"Yes."

"Did he tell you when he was going to leave her?" I asked.

"Whenever we talked about it, he would just say, 'Soon.'"

"Did you ever fight about it?" Lint asked.

"Yes, sometimes, but more so lately."

"Why lately?" Lint asked.

"Because I told him it was either her or me."

"When did you tell him this?" I asked.

"About three weeks ago."

"Did you ever see Doug with a second cell phone," I asked. "Maybe one his wife didn't know about?"

"Yes. He had two cell phones. He said the second one was for work."

"Do you know where that second cell phone is now?" Lint asked.

"I assume Doug has it."

We questioned Oksana for another twenty minutes or so and left. It seemed like she was telling the truth, and if Doug Oliver had something to do with his wife's death, she didn't know about it.

"On our way back to the station, Lint said, "Two hundred and fifty thousand dollars would go a long way in Costa Rica."

"It sure would," I responded.

"You're thinking Doug Oliver killed his wife, aren't you?"

"That's what I'm thinking."

"How does the sexual harassment claim figure into this?"

"I'm thinking it was just a story."

"That's what I'm thinking," Lint agreed. "A story to justify Ron Mosley being in that house."

"But why did he really go to the house, and why did Jennifer Oliver end up dead?" I asked.

"That's the $64,000 question," said Lint.

I dropped Lint back at the station, jumped in my truck, and headed home. On the way home I stopped at Bi-Lo and grabbed a box of Betty Crocker white cake mix and a can of Pillsbury chocolate frosting. I hoped I would be able to talk Bree into baking a cake.

Chapter Nineteen

I had a piece of cake—that I had to bake myself—and a cup of coffee for breakfast and headed to work. Bree had left for work two hours before me. She had asked if I wanted her to make me some breakfast before she left. I told her no, that I would make myself something. She informed me that cake wasn't really a breakfast food. I told her I knew that. She made me promise I wouldn't eat cake for breakfast. I promised her I wouldn't, and then waited until she left to eat it.

When I got to work there was a note on my desk that said NADINE PROCTOR, 41, 1901 MADISON DRIVE, APT-C. At the bottom of the note was a smiley face with some Xs and Os. *Classic Perkins*, I thought.

I stowed my 9mm in the top drawer of my desk and sat down. I turned on my monitor, and typed Nadine Proctor into the search bar of the State Crime Data Base.

Nadine had been arrested for shoplifting in 1995, and then again in 2000. She was arrested for drunk and disorderly in 2001, 2007, and 2009. She did ninety days in the J. Reuben Long Detention Center for assault in 2017, and was still on probation. *No wonder Nadine hated cops,* I thought. *We've hassled her her whole life.*

I printed out two copies of Nadine's rap sheet; one I put in the Jennifer Oliver file, and the other I folded and put in my back pocket.

Lint walked through the door. "Mornin'," he said.

"Mornin'," I responded.

Lint walked directly to the coffee table and grabbed a Krispy Kreme out of the box and shoved it into his mouth.

"Bite-sized?" I asked.

"Hunthisis," he replied.

I watched as he chewed and prepared his coffee. It was so nice to have the old Avis Lint back. That six months he spent as a health nut, dropping pound after pound, was torture. He hadn't gained all the weight back, but he had put some of it back on. I didn't care if Lint was fat or not. I just wanted him to always be larger than me. Does that make me a prick? Yes. Do I care if that makes me a prick? Hell no!

"You want a cup of coffee?" Lint asked.

"Yes, please," I said.

He made mine black and delivered it to my desk. "You want a donut?"

"No thanks. I already ate breakfast."

"What did you have?"

"Um … eggs, bacon, and toast," I lied.

Lint sat his cup on his desk and stowed his weapon in his top drawer. "What's on the agenda for today?" he asked, putting his feet up on the desk.

"Get your goddamn feet off the desk!" said Merle.

Lint jumped, spilling his coffee down the front of his navy-blue dress shirt. "Dammit."

"You are funny," I chortled.

"Where we at?" Merle asked.

"We're headed over this morning to speak with Ron Mosley's sister-in-law," I said.

"What's she got?"

"Nothing yet," I said. "Just want to get her take on Ron, see if she thinks he's the wonderful man everyone else says he is."

Merle clapped his hands together loudly and said, "Then let's get going."

"You gotta run me home to get another shirt," Lint said, as we pulled out of the parking lot.

"You have to start bringing some extra shirts to work," I said.

"That's what Bertie says."

I pulled to the curb in front of Bertie's place, which I guess is also Lint's place now. "Hurry up," I said.

Lint jumped out of the car and did his best impression of someone running up a driveway. When he returned he was wearing a pink dress shirt. He opened the door and climbed in. "What do you think?" he asked.

"About what?" I said.

"The shirt."

"It's pink."

"Yeah. It's not a color I would usually pick out for myself, but Bertie says it looks good on me."

"If you were wearing Wayfarers and beating a drum you would look just like the Energizer Bunny, only fatter."

"You're a prick."

"Am I?"

"Does it look that bad?"

"Yes. You look like an idiot."

"Take me back," Lint said, "and I'll change."

"Too late," I said. "You'll just have to suffer through it."

I took a right onto Twentieth Avenue, and the next left onto Madison Drive.

Nadine Proctor lived in a four-unit brick apartment building almost directly behind the trailer park where the deaf guy painted Lint's face. I pulled the Charger off the street and partway onto the white crushed stone that separated the street from a landscaped garden area. The garden bed was dark mulch with flowers, shrubs, and a few palmettos scattered about in no particular design. A white stone path led from the street to each front door.

We walked up the path that lead to unit C, the stone crunching beneath our shoes. I knocked on the door and reached for my badge.

Nadine opened the door. She looked rough. "Whadda y'all want?" she asked, her eyes squinting against the morning sunshine. "I work nights and I'm trying to sleep, and you—hey, I know you two. You was at my sisters."

"*Ding-ding!*" said Lint, informing Nadine of her correct answer. "We need to come in and ask you a few questions."

"Y'all got a warrant?" Nadine asked.

"Nadine," I said, "you're still on probation. You know we don't need a warrant."

"You gonna back up and let us in," Lint asked, "or are we gonna drag your ass down to the station?"

We were fibbing a little. Nadine didn't have to let us in unless we had her probation officer with us, but the average con doesn't know that.

Nadine rolled her eyes. "Bitch-ass cops," she mumbled, and backed up. "Welcome to my humble abode, massa. Please, do come in." Nadine bowed and waved us in.

"Cut the shit, Nadine," said Lint.

The front door entered into the living room, and a wide doorway beyond that led to the kitchen/dining area. All the floors were off-white ceramic tiles with brown grout. The walls and ceilings were all painted white. The only furniture in the living room was a sofa and a coffee table being used as a TV stand. There were no pictures on the walls, and the windows had no curtains, only mini-blinds. In one corner of the living room were a few U-Haul boxes. There were also boxes in the dining area.

"You just move in?" Lint asked.

"No. I lived here three years now," said Nadine. "Why you ask?"

"Well, there's—no reason."

Nadine walked into the kitchen and we followed. "Sit," she said, pointing at the metal folding chairs around the table. "I have coffee. You want some?"

"No thanks," I said.

"Yes, please," said Lint.

Nadine turned around and gave him her Aunt Esther look. She hadn't expected either one of us to say yes. Sighing and cursing under her breath, she opened the cupboard door above the coffee maker and pulled out a brown Dunkin Donuts mug. She poured it three quarters full and shoved it in Lint's face. She didn't ask him if he wanted sugar or cream.

"Thank you," said Lint. He blew into the mug, and tasted it. "It's cold." His face looked like he'd just licked a turd.

"Yeah, so?" said Nadine. "It's from yesterday. I ain't pourin' perfectly good coffee down the drain."

"Can you put it in the microwave at least?"

"No, but you can." Nadine waved her arm toward the microwave.

"Never mind," Lint said and set the cup on the table.

"You best not waste that, fool."

Lint picked it back up and took a sip. He cringed as he swallowed.

"So, what y'all want?" Nadine demanded.

"Your brother-in-law," I said.

"What about him?"

"His coworkers and his wife all say he's a wonderful man."

Nadine cackled mirthlessly. "You shittin' me, white boy? He ain't no wonderful man. He's all high and mighty 'cause he go to college. My sister thinks she the cat's shit since she marry him. Shit, they ain't nothin'. He sure ain't nothin' ... but dead. Women always be gettin' excited about nothin' ... then marryin' him."

I had heard that quote somewhere before. Nadine couldn't have used it any better. I glanced over at Lint, he was still choking down his cup of cold mud, so I figured he was too preoccupied to ask any questions. "What exactly is your problem with him ... other than him thinking he's the cat's shit?"

"That man's a dog," said Nadine. "He's always had some ho on the side. Thelma think he's all that. Like I say, he ain't shit. He been tryin' to get up on me about once a month since I known him."

"You ever let him on?" asked Lint.

"Wouldn't you like to know, fat boy?"

"Yes, I would," said Lint.

"Shee-it, I never let that man touch me. I even told Thelma about it once. She ask Ron and he say he was just jokin'. Just jokin' my ass. You saw them flowers. Why you think Ron buy those flowers for Thelma? 'Cause he feelin' guilty 'bout somethin', that's why."

"How come you're the only one who seems to know about this side of Ron?" I asked

"Because you askin' the wrong people. You askin' his wife. She thinks he all that. You ask the people he work with. They all love Ron. He ain't stupid. He don't shit where he eats."

"What do you mean?" asked Lint.

"He probably never say nothin' to any of those women he works with, so they all think he's wonderful Ron."

"You think he killed Jennifer Oliver?" I asked.

"Shit no!" said Nadine. "Ron may be a lot of things, but he ain't no killer. He wasn't no violent man. He might have been stickin' it to that white woman, but he wouldn't of killed her."

"Thank you, Ms. Proctor," I said, and handed her my card. "If you think of anything else that might help our investigation, please, give me a call."

"Mm-hmm."

Lint downed the remainder of his coffee in one gulp and we left.

"God, that coffee was terrible," Lint said, when we got in the car.

"Then why did you drink it?" I asked.

"I didn't want her to think I was racist."

Usually I have a comeback for every stupid thing Lint says, but this time I was at a loss.

Chapter Twenty

After we left Nadine Proctor's apartment, Lint and I came up with a plan to get Martha Oliver alone so we could question her. We drove up to Little River and parked off the side of the street near the corner of Queens Road and Kings Drive. I pulled out my cell phone and called Doug Oliver.

"Hello?" Doug answered.

"Doug, it's Detective Stellar," I said. "Hey, are you busy?"

"Not really. What's up?"

"I was wondering if you could meet my partner and me over at your house?"

"Uh ... yeah. Is everything okay?"

"Everything is fine, Mr. Oliver. We're just trying to close this case, and my captain wants us to run through how everything went down that night. Just need to dot the i's and cross the t's. You know how it is. As soon as we sign off, I'll send a copy of the report to your wife's life insurance company."

"Yeah, sure thing, Jake. When did you want to meet me?"

"Is now okay?"

"Yeah. Let me throw on some shoes and I'll be right there."

"Thanks, Mr. Oliver." I hung up the phone and turned to Lint. "We don't want to keep the poor guy waiting too long for his money," I said.

"Yeah," Lint agreed. "He's got plane tickets to Costa Rica to purchase."

"I bet Oksana Alexandrova has her bikini packed already."

"You like saying that name, don't you?" said Lint slyly. "I bet you fancy you're James Bond."

Sometimes Lint was too smart for his own good. Sometimes, as in almost never.

We sat there for another ten minutes before Doug Oliver drove by in his Camry. I started the Charger and drove to his sister-in-laws house.

Martha Oliver was a little surprised to see us when she opened the door. "Oh … you just missed Doug," she informed us. "He thought he was supposed to meet you at his place."

"That's weird," said Lint. "We told him we would pick him up."

"I'll call him," Martha said.

"No, that's okay," I said. "We'll catch up with him. Can we speak to you for a second?"

"Sure, I guess."

We followed Martha into the house and sat in the same chairs we had sat in before. I caught Lint searching the countertop for cake.

Martha offered us coffee. This time we both said no.

"What did you want to speak to me about?" Martha asked. She took a seat across from me.

"We wanted to talk to you about Doug and Jennifer's problems," said Lint.

"Oh," said Martha.

"Now that Doug's not here, maybe you could tell us what those problems were," I said.

Martha looked around the room like she was checking for ears. She looked behind her and even stretched her neck to peer down the hall. I wondered if I should check under the table. Finally she returned her attention to me.

"Go ahead, Martha," I said.

"Now, this is just between us," she said.

"Of course," Lint replied.

"The two of them—Doug and Jen—have had a lot of trouble with infidelity."

"Who was the trouble *maker*?" I asked.

"Oh, both of them. He would cheat on her, and she would cheat on him. They were always fighting about it. Doug would run to my husband and complain about Jen, and Jen would run to me every time Doug cheated on her. For a while they even tried ... you know."

I looked at Lint and then back at Martha. "No, I don't know."

Martha placed her open hand beside her mouth and whispered, "An open marriage."

"Oh," I whispered back. "An open marriage."

Martha nodded her head.

"I take it that didn't work either," said Lint.

"No," said Martha. "He was angry if she was seeing someone and he wasn't, and it was the same with her."

I could tell Martha was still holding something back. "Is there anything else about their relationship that you can tell us?" I asked.

"Well, there is this one other thing," she replied.

"What is it?" asked Lint.

"I don't want to say."

"Is this something Doug told you?" I asked.

"No. Doug told my husband, and my husband told me."

"Go ahead, Mrs. Oliver," I said. "There's nothing we haven't heard before."

Martha took one more look around. "He liked to watch her have sex with other men."

"I see. Mrs. Oliver, would it be okay if we took a look around Doug's room?"

"You mean his room here?" she asked.

"Yes."

"Don't you need his permission for that?"

"No," said Lint. "It's your house. We only need your permission."

"Oh." Martha sat there for a second contemplating. "Do you think Doug had something to do with Jennifer's death?" she asked.

"We think it's a possibility," I said.

"Maybe I should call my husband at work," said Martha.

Lint reached over and placed his hand on top of Martha's. "Mrs. Oliver, we realize we're putting you in a difficult situation, but your help could clear an innocent man's name. Ronald Mosley's widow should know that he didn't murder Jennifer Oliver."

"Okay," Martha said, nodding her head. "But please make it quick."

"We will," Lint said.

The three of us got up from the table, and Martha showed us to Doug's bedroom.

"Can you please wait out in the hall, Mrs. Oliver?" I requested.

Martha backed up and leaned against the wall. The look on her face said she already regretted her decision.

I started with a cabinet door in a small bookcase, and Lint looked under the mattress and under the bed. Lint moved to the nightstand, and I checked out a six-drawer chest of drawers.

When I got to the bottom drawer I announced, "Here it is."

Lint turned around, and Martha stepped into the room.

"Get me an evidence bag," I said.

Lint hurried from the room and returned minutes later with a small clear evidence bag and a pair of rubber gloves. I put one of the gloves on my right hand and picked up the pre-paid flip-phone and slid it into the bag. I held up the bag to and showed it to Martha.

"Have you ever seen this cell phone before?" I asked.

Martha shook her head no.

I turned the bag to inspect the phone. There was a smudge of what looked like blood on the removable back plate.

We spent another ten minutes searching the room, but found nothing else.

"Mrs. Oliver, Doug is going to be pretty upset when he finds out this cell phone is missing," I told her. "I'm going to put a unit out front until we get it checked for prints."

Martha put her hand over her mouth. She nodded her head again.

"Are you going to be okay?" I asked.

"Yes," she said. "Is it okay if I call my husband now?"

"No," I said. "We would rather you didn't"

"Why not?" asked Martha.

"Just let him come home from work on his own. We can't risk having him inform Doug that we were here."

Martha looked up at the clock. "He'll be home for lunch in a half hour any way," she said.

"Then you can explain everything to him when he gets here," Lint said.

"He's going to be mad at me."

"You did the right thing," I said.

My cell phone rang. It was Doug Oliver.

"Stellar," I answered.

"Hey, Jake," he said. "It's Doug Oliver. Were you still going to meet me here at my place?"

"Yeah, Mr. Oliver. We're running a little late. Wait right there. We'll be there in fifteen minutes."

"You got it," he said.

Lint called for a unit and I called Perkins. I thought it would be best if Perkins waited inside with Martha and her husband. I figured it would also be best if Perkins explained everything to Martha's husband, rather than him hearing it from her.

We waited until Perkins and the uniform arrived. We quickly got them up to speed and walked outside.

"You take Perkins' Crown Vic," I told Lint, "and head over to Doug's place. You keep him there until I call you."

"Roger that," Lint replied.

I jumped in the Charger and called Chavez on my way to Weatherwood Drive. I told him to meet me at Oksana Alexandrova's place and to bring a wire for Oksana to wear.

Chapter Twenty-One

I parked in the driveway and walked up to the front door. I knocked and pressed the doorbell button. There was no need to show my badge.

"Yes?" said Oksana.

"May I come in, Ms, Alexandrova?" I asked.

She stared at me for a second, and looked around me. "Are you alone?" she asked.

"Yes. My partner is with Doug, at Doug's house."

"Is he being arrested?"

"Not yet."

"Is he going to be arrested?"

"With your help."

"I don't want him to be arrested. I love him."

"I understand your feelings, but he'll be charged eventually; we just need your help to do it today."

"He didn't kill his wife." Her tone was adamant.

"Then wear a wire and prove it."

"A wire?"

Chavez and a female officer pulled up in a plain white van. He drove it around the cul-de-sac and parked at the curb, facing in the opposite direction. A patrol car with two uniformed officers pulled up behind him.

"I need you to wear a recording device, Ms. Alexandrova. We need you to get Doug to tell you what he did. We also want to put a recording device on your cell phone."

Oksana gazed past me at the officers getting out of their vehicles. "What makes you so sure Doug killed his wife? Doug told me the coroner said the other man did it."

"We think Doug purchased a cell phone for his wife to give to Ron Mosley, a cell phone that couldn't be traced to Ron. We think Jennifer called Ron the night of her murder, on that cell phone, and asked him to come over."

"But Ron was harassing Jennifer," said Oksana. "Why would she ask him to come over?"

"We think that was a story made up by Doug and his wife. We don't believe Ron ever harassed anyone. We think their original plan was to sue the school for firing her."

"You're saying he lied to me."

"He lied to everyone. You, Jennifer, and Ron Mosley."

"He told me he loved me. He told me he never cheated on his wife before me. He said we were soul mates."

"That's also not true, Oksana," I explained. "Doug and Jennifer had an open marriage. You weren't the first, just the first he would kill for."

Oksana dropped her head and stared at the floor. "I'll do it."

"Thank you."

"I'll prove that Doug didn't kill her."

I turned and waved Chavez and the others up to the house.

Chapter Twenty-Two

It only took Chavez about an hour to set things up. Oksana was wearing a wire taped to her chest, and a listening device was attached to her cell phone. Chavez parked the van two houses down the street. We parked the Charger and the patrol car one street over, on Water Tower Road. The vehicles were parked out of sight and off the road behind a fence and some pines, at the back of the Alexandrova property. The two male uniforms waited at the cars. The female uniform—Janet Atkins—stayed at the house with us.

"Just talk normal, Ms. Alexandrova," Chavez said. "This microphone will pick up everything the two of you say."

"Okay," she said.

I pulled out my cell and called Lint.

"Hello?" Lint said.

"Were all set here."

"You got it."

I hung up.

"Remember," Chavez coached Oksana, "speak normally. Tell him the cops were here, and they were asking you a bunch of questions."

"Tell him we think he killed his wife," I said.

"Act frantic, and confused," said Janet.

"I am confused," said Oksana, nearly in tears. "Confused and scared."

"You have nothing to be scared about," Janet told her. "We'll be right outside."

"Call Doug," I said, handing Oksana her phone.

Oksana took the phone and dialed.

"Hey, baby!" Doug said. "What's up?"

"The police were here again," said Oksana.

"What did they want?" Doug asked.

"They were asking me a bunch of questions."

"Like what?"

"I need to see you, Doug."

"I'll be right there, baby."

Oksana hung up.

"Great job," said Janet. She gave Oksana a hug. "Everything will be fine."

The three of us left the house and hurried down the street to the van.

Doug pulled into Oksana's driveway ten minutes later.

"It's show time," said Chavez.

The three of us sat in the back of the van with head phones on. I keyed the mic on my walkie. "The subject is inside the house. Stand by."

"What's the matter, baby?" Doug asked.

"The cops think you killed Jennifer," said Oksana.

"They told you that?"

"Yes. They said you set that Ron guy up."

"I was just at my house with that fat detective. He acted as though everything was fine."

Chavez and I looked at each other and chuckled.

"Fat detective," Chavez whispered.

"I wonder who he's talking about?" said Janet.

We chuckled again.

"I can't wait to tell him," I said.

"They said you made up the whole story about that guy harassing Jennifer," said Oksana.

"Why would we make it up?" asked Doug. "That doesn't make any sense."

"So it would make everyone think he did it."

"Christ! I can't believe this is happening."

"Doug, please tell me, did you kill Jennifer?"

"No!"

"They said they think I helped you."

"Nice one," I whispered.

"Why would they think you helped me?"

"Did you do it, Doug? You have to tell me. If you did it, I know you only did it so we could be together, but I can't be with you if you don't tell me the truth."

"Stand by," I said.

"Please, Doug, tell me the truth."

"I had to," Doug said.

Janet took off her headphones.

"Wait," I said. "Not yet."

"I had to do it," said Doug. "I wanted to be with you."

"Why, Doug?"

"What are you doing?" Doug asked. "What is that?"

"Go! Go! Go!" I shouted.

Chavez and I whipped off our headphones. We all jumped out of the van. Janet was to the door first. She tried the knob; it was locked. Chavez brought his knee up to his chest and kicked the door open, hitting it so hard the knob lodged in the sheetrock wall behind it.

"Police!" I shouted.

The two uniforms were through the rear entrance seconds behind us.

Doug stood in the middle of the kitchen. He had one arm around Oksana's waist. In his other hand was a butcher knife he had pressed against Oksana's throat. The front of Oksana's shirt was ripped open, revealing the microphone taped to her chest.

"Put it down, Doug," I said.

Oksana's eyes were locked onto Janet's. "Help me," she murmured.

"Shut up!" Doug shouted.

"Put down the knife, Doug," said Chavez.

I drew my weapon. "There's only one of two ways you leave this house, Doug: in cuffs, or in a body bag."

"I'll kill her," Doug warned.

"I don't care," I replied. "If two murderers die today, I'll sleep just as good tonight."

"She didn't kill anyone!" Doug hollered.

Tears streamed down Oksana's face, and her entire body trembled.

"Don't pretend you care about her, Doug," I said. "You're holding a knife to her throat."

Doug eased his grip.

"Just put down the knife, Doug," said Janet calmly.

Doug slowly took his hand away from Oksana's neck and dropped the knife.

Oksana ran to Janet.

The two uniforms moved in and cuffed Doug Oliver.

"You have the right to remain silent," one of them began, in a monotone voice. "Anything you say can and will be used against you ..."

Chapter Twenty-Three

"He actually said 'the fat detective?'" Lint asked.

"That's what he said," I replied.

"What a dick."

Lint and I walked down the hall. I opened the door to the interrogation room. One of the uniforms who had been at Oksana's house was standing in the room babysitting Doug Oliver.

Doug sat in a metal folding chair with one hand cuffed to a steel rod that was fastened to the top of a Formica tabletop.

Lint gave Doug a dirty look as he entered the room. "Fat detective, huh?" he said.

I tossed my yellow legal pad on the table and nodded to the uniform; he left the room and shut the door behind him.

"I'm sorry," said Doug.

I looked at Lint with feigned confusion, and then back at Doug. "You don't owe me an apology Doug." I decided to dispense with the formalities.

"I just mean … I should have told you the truth from the beginning."

"The truth?" I asked.

Lint pulled out a chair across from Doug and sat down. I remained standing. I took a ballpoint pen from my front pocket and began clicking it open and closed, repeatedly. The annoying sound seemed to unnerve Doug, which was exactly what I was going for.

"She was always cheating on me," said Doug. "When I came home from work and caught her with Ron Mosley, I just snapped."

"Doug, I didn't come in here to ask you what happened; I already know what happened."

"You do?"

"Yes. Your wife was fired from her job at the high school because of her poor attendance record."

"No, it was because—"

"Shut up, Doug," said Lint. "Let the man talk."

"After Jennifer was fired, you and her cooked up the sexual harassment claim. You thought if you could make it look like Ron Mosley raped her, then everyone would believe you. You could show them the diary—and by the way, the diary's juvenile design is another big strike against you—and how she documented the harassment, just like you showed it to me. You could say that Jennifer told her superiors at work numerous times about the harassment, and now they were trying to cover it up. Everyone would believe the poor white woman who had just been raped over the big black man and the school system. Your plan was to sue the school, probably for millions."

Doug sat quietly as I spoke. The color slowly drained from his face.

"You bought the cell phone and gave it to your wife. You told her to give it to Ron, so the two of them could communicate in private. We have the cell phone, by the way. We found it in a dresser drawer at your brothers. Very sloppy of you, Doug."

"There's a bloody fingerprint on the back," Lint said. "We think it might be Ron Mosley's."

I clicked away at the pen. I could just about see the wheels turning in Doug Oliver's head as he cursed himself for his carelessness.

"We don't know exactly when Jennifer and Ron's affair started," I continued. "We know it started sometime after she was fired. I'm sure you know when that was, though. After all, you knew about their affair, because it was all part of the plan. As a matter of fact, according to your brother, you liked to watch Jennifer do the wango-tango with other men."

Doug was now sweating, and his face was as white as a sheet. I went on:

"The night Jennifer was murdered, she called Ron on the cell phone and asked him to come over. Right after she called him, she called you. You went home after work and caught the two of them in bed together, just like you were supposed to. It was a lot like the other times you watched them have sex, only this time Jennifer wanted to try something new. She wanted Ron to tie her hands and feet to the bed post. She wanted it a little rougher this time. She asked him to bite her breasts, and to force himself on her. After you made sure everything was happening the way it was supposed to, you went to the pantry and got your pistol, and called 911. You returned to the bedroom and told Ron to get off your wife."

"I bet that surprised the shit out of ol' Ron," said Lint.

"Then you put three rounds into his chest," I said. "And that's how it was supposed to end, but it didn't, did it, Doug? Because unbeknownst to Jennifer, your girlfriend, Oksana, had given you an ultimatum days earlier."

"It was her or Jennifer," said Lint.

"And you chose Oksana," I said.

"You walked back into the kitchen," said Lint, "got the knife, and stabbed your wife repeatedly, while standing at her bedside."

"That's why the knife wounds were horizontal and not vertical," I said. I was still clicking my pen, much to Doug's vexation.

"And why there were so many hesitation wounds," said Lint. "Like if somebody was stabbing a loved one."

"Not like somebody who was stabbing someone in a fit of rage, like you said Ron Mosley was doing."

"There was also the bottle of wine," said Lint. "Sure, maybe Doug needed a drink to get up the nerve to commit murder, but it seemed odd that Jennifer needed a drink as well."

"Yeah, the wine got me thinking too," I admitted. "But there was one thing that stood out to me."

Lint nodded his head. "Me too."

I tore a sheet of paper off the top of the legal pad and handed it to Lint along with the pen. "Just for fun, write down what it was that got you thinking, partner," I said.

Lint covered the paper with his arm as he wrote, like a kid not wanting another student to see his test answers. When he finished writing, he folded the paper in half.

Doug had watched him the whole time with the intensity of a chess player. He looked at me expectantly.

"Ron's folded clothes on the chair," I said. "Let's see your answer, Lint."

Lint unfolded the paper and showed it to Doug and me. He grinned proudly. Written on the paper was RON'S FOLDED CLOTHES.

"Nice!" I said; the two of us high-fived. "If you had just thrown Ron's clothes on the floor, I never would have questioned it."

"Yeah," Lint put in, "A guy who's about to rape and murder a woman doesn't usually take the time to fold his clothes neatly and place them on a chair, the way Ron did."

"Maybe I need a lawyer," said Doug.

"We could go that route," I said.

"Or you could just admit what you did," said Lint.

"You see, Doug, if you just go ahead and tell us the truth now, it could mean the difference between life in prison and the death penalty."

Ron glared at the legal pad as I slid it slowly across the table to him. Lint laid the pen on top of the pad.

"Start writing, Doug," I said.

We waited in silence as Doug decided what to do. Finally, after thirty or forty seconds, he picked up the pen and started writing his statement.

The End

Coming Soon:

From the Tales of Dan Coast
Neighborhood Watch

From the Tales of Dan Coast
Another Mother

ALSO BY RODNEY RIESEL

From the Tales of Dan Coast Series

Sleeping Dogs Lie
Ocean Floors
The Coast of Christmas Past
Ship of Fools
Double Trouble
Most Likely to Die
Deadly Moves
On the Wagon
No Enemies Here

Jake Stellar Series

North Murder Beach
Beach Shoot
When Death Returns
The Obedience of Fools
Dead in the Water

The Dunquin Cove Series

The Man in Room Number Four
Return to Dunquin Cove
Local Hero

www.ingramcontent.com/pod-product-compliance
Lightning Source LLC
Chambersburg PA
CBHW071918220626
47052CB00002B/406